MOTHER

Marina Perezagua

Translated from the Spanish by
Robin Myers

akoya

LONDON

'Some blows in life, they're so heavy . . . I don't know.'
César Vallejo, tr. Yvette Siegert

'O God, thy sea is so great and my boat is so small.'
Anonymous fisherman's prayer

To every mother who has ever given birth alone.
To my great-grandmother Dolores.
To Adrianne, our nurse.

For my daughter Estrella.

By the time you're old enough to
read your mother's edges,
some will have already scratched you.
All my edges, broken or polished, are made of love.
We met naked.
That's how I write these words to you.
That's how you should read them.

I

PLEA

This is the plea that became the bedrock for this book:

> I want my daughter alive:
> alive no matter what.
> Alive as a girl,
> as a stain,
> as a scab.

II

CONTEXT

My mother has tried to take away everything I've ever accomplished. Either that or she's mocked it. How could I be so stubborn as to think she'd let me carry my pregnancy to term without incident? When I got pregnant, I swore she'd never take my baby away. I remember it perfectly. I wanted to protect my child so badly that my words made her into a possession. *Mum, you'll never take this away from me,* I said to myself. What happened between this steadfast vow of protection, and the sinister spectacle of my mother feigning asphyxiation that would bring my tragedy to pass? It was stupid of me to think, yet again and for no good reason, that my mother would ever protect me.

Two prostitutes who lived in the same house gave birth almost at the same time. One night, one of the women accidentally rolled over in bed and smothered her baby. She picked up her dead child, slipped into her housemate's room and swapped him for the living one. When the second woman woke up to breastfeed, she realised the baby beside her was dead – and also that he wasn't her son. The women fought until King Solomon intervened and issued his famous verdict, recounted as follows in the first Book of Kings:

> Then the other woman said, 'No! But the living one is my son, and the dead one is your son.'

> And the first woman said, 'No! But the dead one is your son, and the living one is my son.'
>
> Thus they spoke before the king . . .
>
> Then the king said, 'Bring me a sword.' So they brought a sword before the king. And the king said, 'Divide the living child in two, and give half to one, and half to the other.'
>
> Then the woman whose son was living spoke to the king, for she yearned with compassion for her son; and she said, 'O my lord, give her the living child, and by no means kill him!'
>
> But the other said, 'Let him be neither mine nor yours, but divide him.'
>
> So the king answered and said, 'Give the first woman the living child, and by no means kill him; she is his mother.'

My daughter and I are what could have happened if King Solomon had used his sword: life divided, flesh sundered. When it comes to the flesh of her flesh, my mother is indifference incarnate. She would have settled for the dead child, or half a child. Solomon's judgement, as we know it today, would have been very different. My mother's taste is a bitter one. I don't remember it, but I'm sure.

My mother committed infanticide, or tried to. I'll come back to this later. I only mention it now because I want you to know about it from the very beginning. Whoever you are, tuck this into the back of your mind as you start to read: my mother triggered my daughter's premature birth, nearly four months before my due date.

My mother sent me into early labour. And then she left.

It was a day at the beach.

One of my earliest memories involves a gash. I burst out of my bedroom in tears, yelping 'My bottom is broken!' I couldn't hear anything my mother tried to say. I was convinced: I'd touched my bottom and felt the rift between the cheeks. It was the first time I'd ever perceived this part of my body. My mother pulled down her trousers and underwear and tried to reassure me by showing me hers; it looked just like mine. All this achieved was that, at least for a while, I believed we were the only two people on earth with broken bottoms. This actually comforted me more than the idea of sharing a physical feature with all of humankind. It soothed me to think that my mother and I, just the two of us, were united – if only by a crack, by a ditch.

Today that ditch is the bed of dry leaves at the foot of a cliff I push my mother over. She wrenched my daughter from my womb before it was time. I dream of beating her. I'm not ashamed to admit it; I beat my mother in a rage, then shove her into the void. If I didn't have to spend my days hovering beside an incubator, maybe these dreams would come true.

The last time I saw my mother while feeling mentally and physically well was just a few days ago. At the beach. The dunes must still be marked by those hours of warmth and plenitude, mixed with particles of incipient disaster. I know I left something important there. Something of value, something I need. A gold piece that none of those amateur diggers who turn up with their metal detectors at sundown can ever find. I suspect it's forgiveness. But I haven't found it yet. The beach, that beach in particular, is endless.

III

25 WEEKS AND 5 DAYS

22.9 OUNCES

(Resurrection)

My baby's skin is so fine and translucent, and flushed so red, that she could be raw. My unfinished baby, born at the limit, so the doctors repeated, as they whisked her away before I could even see her, their voices diluting deep into the corridors: 'Born at twenty-five weeks, the limit of viability.'

A few hours later, they explained what this limit meant: babies born before week twenty-eight are considered micropreemies. Once outside their mother's womb, they're predicted to survive minutes, hours at most. Or, in most parents' best-case scenario, they may keep gestating for months in an incubator, laid out on the pristine sheets of dreaded consequences.

As they swept me down the hospital corridors, I heard one of the many voices swirling above my stretcher repeat a command: 'We're going to try to save them both.'

In the operating room, the doctors and nurses bustled across the seething floor of reality, a tornado's eye that narrowed around us. Every once in a while I felt their frightened glances. It was a strange sensation; their worry, apparently impossible to hide, was flattering somehow. Everyone was taking care of us. Nobody was thinking about anything but saving us, both of us. They'd said so: 'We're going to try to save them both.' At that moment, none of these people had a family or a schedule; none were hungry or afflicted by any other woes. A nurse with thick, wavy red hair squeezed my hand in reassurance, and when I felt her about to pull away, I tightened my grip. She didn't try to leave again. She understood that this was going to be her most important job in the whole process.

I had an ultrasound to make sure my baby was viable.

In the state of New York, doctors are obligated to revive a baby starting in week twenty-six, regardless of the parents' wishes. But this depends on its viability. That is, if the baby is seriously underweight for their gestational age, some doctors let parents participate in the decision. I was in what's known as the 'grey area', a dubious realm that depends on an agreement between a mother with no medical knowledge and several doctors who can't predict how the hundreds of preemie-related variables will play out.

They lobbed the decision at me and asked, should my daughter prove unviable, if I'd want the manoeuvres of revival to be performed once she was born. She might live for a few minutes, they said, in which case we'd have the chance to meet each other. I don't think I answered, because someone repeated the question with a different word: 'resuscitation'. I was slow to reply, my thoughts subsumed in an incomprehensible conversation with myself. 'Resuscitation'. I'd never associated this word with a baby, much less with the daughter who'd been moving around inside me just hours before as I swam, weightless, in a patch of the Atlantic Ocean. Old people get resuscitated. The dead get resuscitated. The gods I don't believe in. That's how it should be.

At last, my mind resumed external communication, and I replied: 'Yes. Revive her.'

And then I repeated to myself, fearing I was too weak to be heard: 'Yes. Revive her.'

And I heard it again: 'All right. We're going to try to save them both.'

If my mother had been with me, if she'd wanted or been able to worry about my daughter, to love her, then maybe I could have started loving her again too. But she left, as usual, and didn't come back until the next day. She was capable of spending twenty-four hours without knowing whether at least one of us, her daughter or her granddaughter, had made it through the night. As if that weren't enough, I was suddenly slammed with the weight of all the ways she'd abandoned me since I was a child.

When my mother left the hospital in those first uncertain hours, she also exited the possibility I'd held so dear: that I would be able to shed the loneliness I'd worn like a garment my whole life. A different dress for every day of the week, and an especially lonely one for holidays, for Christmas, for every birthday I'd never celebrated.

By the time they brought me into the operating room, my liver and kidneys were failing. My blood pressure was 220/160 mmHG. I suddenly found myself surrounded by doctors and health professionals. A woman's voice said I might start convulsing and urged me to trust her team. I'm not sure exactly when, but I passed into a nightmarish kind of limbo that would last for days, weakened by the magnesium sulphate I was administered to lower the risk of stroke. I didn't even have the strength to change position or make certain gestures, and my thinking turned anachronistic: if a doctor answered a question I'd asked, I'd already forgotten what it was, so any reply felt enigmatic, even menacing. And my baby wasn't with me. My milk didn't come in. 'All that matters is that you stay alive,' they tell you, but your hormones and your instinct seize with the need to have your infant suckling at your breast. Not that she'd survive on me alone. In the event that she lived, thanks to many other factors that didn't depend on me at all, she'd need the milk of another woman, or industrial milk. She'd also need a miracle. Maybe someday I won't believe this, but for now I still do; my body is a failure.

My mother hovered on the threshold between my life and my death, blithe and nonchalant as she'd always been towards me. She was there: she witnessed the urgency of the doctors, who alerted her to my dire state when I was in the operating room. It couldn't have been abstract to her. Yes, my mother was on the threshold between my life and my death, and at the same time she wasn't there, as she proved by deciding to leave. My mother was the light at the end of the tunnel, moving away like a train in the cold night, as I fought my way back, dragging myself towards life like a lizard with its legs cut off.

I felt an intense pressure in my abdomen, and everything happened very fast, the contractions were merciless, one after another, the crest of a tsunami threatening to sweep my daughter and me away, both of us far too small for a wave so great. I heard a bellow of pain, like a cow. It was me. A guttural surrender of strength. I always imagined the screams of childbirth as shrill, sharp, but now I know they're not, or not always. I, at least, shouted into myself, as if towards my vagina, not up to the sky. No, not the sky. The sky offered me nothing but fear.

The medical team urged me to push. I'm physically quite strong, but I found myself terrified of bringing my daughter into the world so soon. I knew I wasn't pushing as hard as I could. A nurse held a mirror between my legs so I could see the baby's head peeking out; I suppose she was trying to encourage me. A new contraction hit and I pushed again, and although I was still holding back a little, I saw her emerge like a sphere, crowning in the bloody mists. I felt so overwhelmed that I burst into tears, which instantly sapped my strength; when the next contraction came, I couldn't even push. All my energy was drained by the intensity of glimpsing the tiny head I'd created, so blindly and so fast. It seemed like magic. How does a head get made?

It was crucial that she come out as soon as possible. The doctors kept cheering me on, but their insistence was so resolute that it felt forceful, even threatening. Like an order. I had to do this, they said, I had to avoid a C-section, preemies born vaginally have higher chances of survival. So I did: I held my breath and pushed as hard as I could, just once, but it felt like an endless passage, and I felt a burning, a stretching, a breaking, a tearing at my tissues. And then my little girl came out.

I think I heard a cry, faint as a kitten's, then nothing. Silence. I glimpsed her through the fog in my eyes. Her body looked smooth. I couldn't see her face, but something that must have been her arms and legs dangled alongside the doctor who held her, wrapped her in a blanket and vanished from my sight.

It's hard to recount a premature birth, because you're there and you're not. You watch through your daughter's closed eyes, because that's where you are – in her – and this means watching in a state of absolute uncertainty. Or maybe it's fear. Maybe we've misunderstood fear as a personal, subjective feeling. Maybe we're wrong. I, at least, feel that fear – and I don't mean only the fear of early labour – is located somewhere else, in someone else; a sensation that belongs to us without belonging to us. That's what makes it so terrifying. Once in a while, you return to yourself and see something, I don't know what, but it's not objective or describable in a way that can show another person what premature childbirth is like. Mine reminds me of an image that's been carved into my memory forever; it comes from the account of someone who survived the underwater earthquake in Sri Lanka that interrupted the day, and the lives, of thirty-five thousand people. Forty per cent were children. Like in a passage from Boccaccio's *Decameron*, that morning thousands of people breakfasted peaceably with their kinsfolk, and hours later, after nightfall, they supped with their ancestors in the other world.

That day, Sonali Deraniyagala tried to flee in a jeep with her husband and two children. In the panic of their escape, it didn't even cross her mind to knock on the door of her parents' room; she just grabbed her kids and ran from one unknown into the next. In the imagination of anyone who's never experienced a tsunami, waves vast as mountains rise up over the ground. But Sonali recounts that their jeep wasn't suddenly pitched aside by a surge of water. Instead, it slowly flooded from below, as if the source of the water wasn't the ocean, but deep inside the earth, welling up from the surface. In Sonali's description, I imagine it more like an apocalyptic deluge than a tsunami per se. Yet the water coursed in the opposite direction: from the earth towards the sky. Maybe that's why I wrote above that my screams during labour didn't want to climb skyward. No, never there: I channelled my strength, my roars, towards my vagina, like a centre of gravity, so all my energy could stay in the tunnel connecting me to life outside, at earth level. Not the sky. Not that journey undertaken by thirty-five thousand dead in Sri Lanka.

That Sunday, Sonali lost her two children – aged five and seven – her husband, her mother, her father and her best friend. But the image I mentioned earlier, the one I always associate with my daughter's birth, is this: her rescuer said that he'd never – not even in the bewilderment of that day and the days that followed – seen anything so strange as the sight of Sonali when he found her. Naked and covered in mud, she wasn't looking for her children, wasn't pleading for help. She just turned in circles, like a little girl wheeling around to make herself dizzy and fall to the ground. Neither the man nor Sonali understood what she was doing. She'd witnessed the chain of her DNA snap forever, the final links scattered and lost in the clay, abandoned from the past (the death of her parents) into the future (the death of her children). No yesterday. No tomorrow. Just a top spinning around herself. In my case, I was a top whose weight, whose gravity, was centred in her vagina, to keep my daughter from flying into the air, into the sky, into the gusts of the void. Maybe that's all I'd be able to do if I survived. Spin and spin until my innards centrifuged me to death. Because I know I'd want to die.[1]

Before I came to the hospital, I was finishing a book, the last pages of which I read on the beach where I'd been happy. They return me to the idea, however fictional or subjective, of finding yourself without DNA, past or future. The book is called *The Soul of an Octopus*, by Sy Montgomery. I remember a few words – a single image – I found especially revealing. They're actually the words of evolutionary biologist Richard Dawkins, and I saved them to my phone, where I keep everything that catches my attention. In the process, I've been able to incorporate literal words or paragraphs from the hospital; everything's right here in a memory card. This writing belongs to this moment: I can expend more or less effort in finding the right form, but I can't help but look. The form depends on my strength, but the content is immediate; there's no such thing as *I'm searching for something to reinforce what I write*. All that matters is survival. I have no time to excavate, only to remember and to want. In any event, the image I mean is Dawkins', as recovered by Mongomery: '"You are standing beside your mother, holding her hand. She is holding her mother's hand, who is holding her mother's hand . . ." Eventually the line stretches three hundred miles long and goes back five million years, and the clasping hand of the ancestor looks like that of a chimpanzee.'[2]

This means that the five-million-year-old mother gave birth to two children: a chimpanzee and me. I'd like to think that I have two mothers: one slouched, hairy and dead; another, still alive, called 'woman'.

When all the squealing machines that slid across the floor went quiet, as well as the voices, the beeping of the monitors, the careening of the medical staff during my hours of labour; when I was sure I heard the faint mewling of a kitten, then nothing, I thought they'd taken my baby away, that they'd all trailed after her in a silent procession. In my weakness and delirium, I drifted into the memory of an afternoon when I was twelve years old. It was Holy Week in Seville, and a friend and I found ourselves suddenly engulfed in a crowd following the Brotherhood of Silence as they marched. There were hundreds of people, but you couldn't hear a soul. No matter what you believed, the experience was overwhelming. How could so many people, children included, agree to fall silent at the same time? And all of a sudden, on a balcony, a woman slashed the silence from the centre of herself, breaking into a sacred saeta song. That's what I did when I thought they'd left me alone and taken my daughter who knows where without even telling me if she was alive, or dead, or somewhere in between. I let out a scream like a lament or a plea for mercy from the crowd. I glanced to my right; contrary to what I thought, I realised there were in fact noises, sounds, everyone was still there, and for some reason it was me who had briefly lost my hearing, or maybe my mind. There, on a stretcher, was my daughter, blurry, and worse: she was still.

'No heartbeat,' I kept hearing, or maybe it was an echo of the only time they said it. And I saw: I watched the process of cardiopulmonary resuscitation performed on a body too small for an adult hand. I don't know why, but the image of a rabbit's heart leapt to mind. My daughter's heart couldn't have been much bigger than that.

A doctor did compressions on her tiny sternum. But he used only his fingers. Just two fingers: that's how little she was. Even so, I felt he was pressing too hard. I caught half a glimpse of what must have been her face, totally covered by a mask, a respirator pumping oxygen into her lungs. But in that moment I didn't even know what it was, just that I couldn't see her face, could barely see her body, and even so, everything I could see of her was too awful for me to endure any more of it.

But it worked. Her heart revved up again. Through the monitors, the room filled with the sound of her heartbeat.

I sang my saeta on Good Friday, when a crucifixion and a death is commemorated. Within seconds, it was Easter Sunday.

I thought: I knew it. I'd spent my entire pregnancy convinced that something terrible was going to happen. In theory, this was irrational, because everything seemed to be going well. That is, until I agreed to have my mother visit me in New York for the weeks before my due date. That's when I knew I'd made a mistake. But not just any mistake: I'd tossed the dice into the air and gambled my daughter's life. All for a chance at reconciliation with my mother. Or maybe, as Sy Montgomery says of herself, I'm just one of those people who harbours a fondness for monsters. The key, she writes, is learning to think like them. Then everything makes sense.

Am I a monster? Maybe I was just overly naive in risking my daughter's life. And risk it I did. Despite the fact that, even before I got pregnant, motherhood meant something very particular to me, completely unrelated to many of the reasons (biological, sociological, voluntary, circumstantial . . .) why a woman might take such a decision. To me, becoming a mother meant refusing to explain myself anymore. It was a kind of insurrection. Making a human being, or so I thought at the time, was a creative act that would grant me autonomy, independence from all the other people who had always centralised my thoughts and actions, like absolutist nation-states. Bringing into the world a life I'd made myself, atom by atom, was a way for me to regain the strength I'd been sapped of since childhood, primarily by my family. Motherhood was my adult response to my own mother's accusation when I was small: 'You're useless.'

Since the first trimester is said to be the most critical, and since I'd already had two miscarriages, I decided to spend those three months in bed. I knew about the benefits of moderate exercise, that a state of total rest can actually be harmful. But I was paralysed by fear. One day, a strange pain lanced through one of my buttocks. I checked myself in the mirror and saw nothing. It puzzled me that there was no sign of the cause, because the discomfort was deep – literally deep, as if the pain began several centimetres under the skin and spread all the way down to my hip bone. Maybe that's why it left no mark; it was still too far from the surface. But it didn't take long to make itself visible. A few days later, I examined myself again, and there it was, a purple sore caused by all the time I'd spent lying down, almost twenty-four hours a day. Heeding my own orders, completely obedient to my own paralysing terror, supported by no medical evidence at all. I knew they were pressure ulcers, also known as bed sores, because I'd seen them on my great-grandmother in the last year of her life. I felt sorry for myself, stricken by how far my voluntary paralysis had gone, by the expanse of my fear: all the way into the ulcer on my skin, on the left side of my body, which is the recommended side for sleeping when you're pregnant. That's what they say: that the body's largest vein, the vena cava, runs along the right side, and it's best to avoid putting pressure on it, which improves the blood supply to the placenta and the flow of oxygen and nutrients to the foetus. So I lived on my left side, gazing towards the same window all day long. Beside the window was a painting; beside the painting, another window. That was my left-side view. That was my only landscape for nearly four months, altered only by the changing light as the hours passed.

Approximately one in three pregnancies end in miscarriage before the twelve-week point. Some of us don't even realise we've had one. If it happens in the first few days, we might mistake it for a more abundant or uncomfortable period. One possible hypothesis for this high percentage of spontaneous abortions is that the body is rehearsing: it prepares itself for carrying to term, as effectively as possible, a pregnancy that will culminate in a living child. This means something different to me, too: before my last pregnancy, I had two other chances to distance myself from my mother as I gestated a life I'd so dearly longed for. And my body didn't take them.

Day two, on my phone, I decide to write to you. I type with one finger. In case you live. I have IVs in both hands. I'm fastened to indecipherable sites and numbers. I don't know where I begin or end. My life flows through the cables hooked up by doctors who defend my survival. But my scant remaining personhood still has a working mind, and it commands my fingers to write to you. Who will tell you about me if I'm the one who doesn't survive? I'm terrified to think that you might grow up without knowing what happened. Or that you might only have access to someone else's version, invariably warped, of this story.

As for the past: in your grandmother's attic, there's a floral-patterned cardboard box. Inside is a diary I kept for many years. You'll find a lot of me in it, countless things I can't tell you now. Time is short. There are photos too, and I hope you'll always keep them with you. Believe me: photos that mark the passage of time in the faces of the people we come from are important. They're maps that show us the way out of the labyrinth, starting from wherever we first began to crawl and extending wherever we decide, more or less, to escape as autonomous beings. When my mother was light and happy, when she was affectionate and could still see me, I learned to walk between the flowering walls of that labyrinth. Life was a game, and my mother was beautiful to me. When I was still very young and she decided to forget she was a mother, to forget I existed, she picked up the map of the labyrinth with me inside it and crumpled it into a ball. She grew ugly and wrinkled. I huddled between the green walls, which closed in on me, and it was only when my own belly began to swell that my body, now powerful, could break through the membranes of maternal lovelessness. My hips, my breasts, my womb were tools of fracture, flight and self-defence; my stretch marks a constellation crowned by the north star, which whispered my freedom. Yes, my baby, you're my way out of the labyrinth. It's a remarkable thing to have someone's help in deciphering the paths towards the exit. Someday, when you too find yourself lost, I'll hope you'll realise how meaningful it is. That's what you've been for me, and what you still are: the interpretation of a world I now love because I can finally understand it.

Writing this, I realise I haven't had time to choose any of the names I've been collecting. What am I supposed to call you as I write these words? First I should introduce myself. Besides being your 'mother', 'mama', or whatever else we're usually called, I have a name of my own: Marina Sonia Perezagua. That's not counting my second surname, the one I've given up – because you know what? I can't make sense of this name stuff in the first place. That's why I'm giving it up. Legally. I know it'll be difficult. I imagine I'll have to roam from office to office, explaining a million times why I don't want my maternal surname, why I'm asking them to take it away. They'll stare as if I'm a traitor. I know those looks. But that's how the world is. Before our eyes have even opened after birth, they've imposed a name on us and carved it into a marble slab. Even if it includes the surname of the person who, in my case, in our case, has tried to kill us somehow. So be it. I want to choose all the names on my gravestone. Aren't I the one who will be buried there? But I'm not who matters right now, and I'm not wasting any time looking for a name. So, if someone reads this and I no longer have a voice or heartbeat, then let them call me 'Mama'. That's that. It's the simplest choice. Let them write something like, 'Here lies Mama, killed by her mother,' with my dates of birth and death. That's enough. But back to the priority: your name. I won't give it to you. Not only because I don't want to press the weight of even a single letter onto the oxygen as it struggles into your lungs, but because at a moment when you can't even choose to live, when you're fighting for a silhouette that resembles a newborn baby's, I want to give you the lightness of *not* tethering you to a name. I'll call you 'Daughter' or 'MyChild' or 'MyBaby', that sort of thing: collective names, weightless, free of connotations.

There's something else. You're still so indeterminate that you remind me of the solitary bird: 'The first, that it flies to the highest point; The second, that it does not suffer company, not even of its own kind; The third, that it holds its beak windward; The fourth, that it has no specific colour; The fifth, that it sings ever so gently.'

MyChild, you meet all of these conditions. You breathe so faintly that it sounds like gentle singing. You have no clear colour. A solitary bird. But you're not alone. You're a beloved bird. Because your name is MyChild and my name is YourMama.

One of the nurses comes in to tell me you're stable, considering your weight and gestational age: the prognosis may not be as negative as they first expected. However, she also warns me that during the first forty-eight hours outside the mother's womb, some preemies experience what the nurses call a 'honeymoon phase'. It might seem like you're all right, you're going to make it, but what's actually happening is that you're exhausting all your available resources to survive a few more hours. A honeymoon. You know neither moon nor honey, MyChild; just a few droplets of tremulous love exuded from my damp skin. They welcome you into the world not with protection, but with the sweat of fear, the furious hormones turning against me.

The neonatologist tells me that preemies are unknown creatures. Each and every one is a just-discovered species, and each responds uniquely to its care and keeping: instant death; death within a few hours; death within the first year; mild, moderate, or severe physical damage for life; survival with no consequences of any kind. Only the last is truly desirable among all these scenarios, all these possible alternatives branching out like mandrake roots beneath your tiny body in unpredictable, mostly foreboding ways. I was granted the right to keep you alive for the remote possibility of a life without motor or neurological difficulties, without any of the dozens upon dozens of problems you might suffer, all rattled off to me by the doctors as if I could still change my mind. Was there any other choice? Even if there were, I want you alive, as I've told you, and I want the doctors to know it:

Alive no matter what.

Alive as a girl.

As a stain.

As a scab.

My room has two beds. I'm still sharing quarters with a woman who gave birth as I did. Like me, she underwent the contractions, the pain, the struggle to push her baby out. Unlike me, she already knew that her baby was dead. We're both recovering from different misfortunes, and in this sense we're marked by yet another difference: she doesn't seem to want to recover. She doesn't speak, cry, or make a sound. She doesn't eat.

This morning, I heard the doctor tell her, 'You have slim chances of birthing a live baby in the future.' He said it as if a live child could replace the dead one. He said it as if she hadn't already forgotten what life is, or the future, or the days of the week. Doctors should learn the language of the dead in medical school. Instead, they learn English.

Despite what the doctor told my roommate, I can't help but wish that another child, another daughter, were waiting for me at home. That might be a reason to keep living if I have to leave this hospital alone. It all feels so contradictory. Why should I need another child to give me a reason to live if I don't want to? I think it's because people who lose a child do indeed want to keep living, we just don't know how. Having another child gives us an excuse that actually isn't one, but seems to be, because caring for them forces us to go on. Then we can say we're staying alive because we have to live for the other child. But that's not true. We don't survive out of altruism or even love. Only a person who wants to live for herself will do so.

When I was little, my mother once told me that people have two or more children in case one dies. She never wanted a second child after me, which led me to conclude that my mother didn't need a replacement; if the wheel of my life were punctured, she'd keep riding along, or she'd get into someone else's car, cranking up the music on a brand-new motorway towards some alluring destination. Still, whenever I remember that last day on the beach, I feel like I'm missing something. Something that might compensate for the actions I condemn and which make me hate her, scorn her, find her as repellent as I do.

My roommate is taking pills to suppress her milk production, but it comes in anyway. We're separated by a curtain that obviously lets me overhear everything. Another doctor, not the one from yesterday, asks if she wants to donate her milk to the hospital's micropreemies. I want to fling back the curtain and beg her not to dam the flow. I wish she could turn into a human cow, tethered to the bed until my daughter has a belly full of breastmilk and can leave this place for good. But I bite my tongue, don't say a word. I speak English, but I've also been teaching myself the language of the dead. If MyChild survives, that's the first language I'll teach her, so she can learn to love and be loved. Who cares about English as a first, second, or final language. I cry out for compassion as the lingua franca.

The woman's husband tries his best to comfort her. But there's not much he can do. Neither he nor anyone can understand the utter depths of her pain. When these mothers leave the hospital, nobody will talk about the babies who were born 'asleep', as the nurses call stillborn infants. Asleep. There are no rituals of solace for children who will never be their mothers' joy. Words are saved for the winners of the first battle: being born alive. Nobody who isn't in our position can grasp the strength it takes to stave off death while forcing one's way into the world. I envy the good fortune of men, who don't birth dead babies. Men who simply disintegrate once and for all at the end of their lives. Only then do they know what it means to be dying. My roommate carried death inside her. And my own death is in your incubator, MyChild, still deliberating whether to emerge – or whether to receive occasional bouquets of flowers laid onto the earth.

It's almost a commonplace, what some mothers say: that the day of their baby's birth was the happiest day of their lives. I don't know if it would have been mine, if I'd gone through childbirth without complications, because that day was the closest I've ever been to death. But like a gift from heaven – maybe the leftovers from some other woman's excess joy, or just a benevolent wink of fate – I did experience several moments I consider among the most radiant I've ever known. It was when I was led into the delivery room. The first thing I saw, to the left, was a cot. A cot much like the one my daughter would nestle in a few months from now, if everything turned out all right. But what moved me most was that someone had prepared it for her. A complete stranger had fitted the mattress with its perfect sanitised sheets, and they'd laid a little sign at the head with my name along with MyChild's, her sex, her weight, her measurements. And best of all: there was a tiny hat with blue and pink stripes, folded as neatly as a delicate origami figurine. Maybe the whole thing looked perfect because it had been mechanically performed; maybe it was a matter of routine for the person in question. But it felt to me like a cot prepared with love, ready to welcome MyBaby. It wasn't the happiest day of my life, but on that day of panic – my confrontation with the void, blood, solitude – there was still room for moments of absolute joy. Her cot. Her pink-and-blue-striped hat. For her. They'd gotten it ready for her. MyChild.

———

There are words I don't want to learn. 'Surfactant', for example. Surfactant is a liquid produced by the lungs starting in week twenty-six of gestation. Its role is to keep the alveoli wet and therefore open: if they dry out, the walls stick together and no air can get in. If a baby is born premature, they may not have been able to produce enough pulmonary surfactant. In that case, the alveoli collapse with every breath and the damaged cells accumulate in the bronchial ducts. The infant struggles to breathe, their oxygen levels plummet. The baby struggles harder and harder to inflate their airways until they eventually tire out and die. Death from exhaustion.

I Google 'surfactant' and discover something else. Until recently, there was only one way to obtain it: specialised workers extracted it from the lungs of certain animals in slaughterhouses. Today, I believe, it's synthetic, although I'm not sure that's the case in all hospitals.

My imagination runs wild with the details I dig up. I picture a scene in an early twentieth-century slaughterhouse, when knowledge of surfactant was limited and the only known way to procure it was through extraction from freshly killed animals. A small, strange man (I don't know how else to describe him; in my mind, he's just a diminutive silhouette with a sick psyche) enters one of the slaughterhouse chambers. The place is dark, rank, frenetic with butchering. The small, strange man makes his way towards a smaller chamber, where he'll perform the extraction of pulmonary liquid. There are pigs and cows strung from enormous rusty hooks: animals whose surfactant-production is similar to that of us humans. The man presses a button that starts to flicker with orange light and makes the corpses file past him like ironed garments at the cleaner's, slipping along the rack. At a certain point, he halts the parade. The bright button goes dark. He selects an animal. First, he meticulously cleans its lungs to eliminate any residues or impurities. Then he places the lungs in a machine specially designed to remove liquid from pulmonary tissue. The machine applies pressure (I can hear the sound) and gentle movements to express the surfactant from the lungs with precision and control. Once the little man has obtained the liquid, he collects and subjects it to a purifying filtration process to ensure it's free of any undesired contaminants. To do so, he uses different techniques and devices that guarantee the quality and sterility of the extracted surfactant. At last, the same man – who, for some reason, I picture carrying out the entire procedure all by himself – carefully stores the liquid in sterile jars, ready for use in the grisly hospitals of the day.

I'm not supposed to get up yet, but this morning a nurse came in and told me she'd return with a wheelchair in a couple of hours; she's going to take me to see MyChild. I can take a few photos if I want. I wasn't sure what to say. She must have known that I wanted this – to see MyBaby – more than anything. But now she's offered me something that hadn't even crossed my mind. And that's when it hit me: they don't think she's going to survive much longer. They're giving me the chance to have a memory of her, while she's still alive.

My roommate has consented to see her son. I eavesdrop. They're going to move her to a room they call the 'bereavement room', which has something they call the 'cuddle cot': a portable cot set with a kind of blanket hooked up to a refrigeration unit. In this way, any visible effects of death will be slowed, so parents have time to say goodbye to their baby. The nurse says the woman can spend hours or even a couple days with him there. A midwife advises her to call other family members, hug the child, take photos of him in different outfits, snip a lock of his hair or take a print of his hands and feet on a special type of paper that the hospital can provide.

So, I'll be left even more alone in this room. While an incubator tries to keep my daughter warm, my roommate can only see her son with the aid of a refrigerated cradle. I don't want to think of that cold as a thin, vaporous line that could separate my present from an imminent future, one in which I too am presented with

MyBaby wrapped in glacial sheets. Sometimes the pain is so intense that I think: It doesn't matter. If she goes, it won't hurt, because I won't let her go alone. If she goes, I'll go with her. I'll be with her every step of the way.

Being a mother doesn't mean you'd give your life for your child, as cliché would have it. It's the kind of truism that gets passed down unthinkingly from generation to generation – or maybe people do think about it, which is worse. To me, being a mother means *having* to give your life for your child, even if you want to live. It's a tragedy, something that can't be changed. I don't think it's a matter of love (although love has a lot to do with it) so much as a different feeling we can't control or name. I've feared death ever since I could grasp the concept of nothingness. I've always thought that I'd do whatever it took to survive, that I wouldn't die for anyone. Now these thoughts are one and the same: I fear death as I always have, and yet, if I had to donate my heart to my daughter or throw myself in front of a moving car to save her, I'd do it without hesitation. Maybe I'd regret it once I was dead, if such a thing were possible, but I'd do it anyway. I don't know what to call this inconsistency. Evolutionary instinct? Mere reproductive programming?

Being a mother is impossible to understand if you don't have children.

Being a mother is impossible to understand if you do have children.

Being a mother can only be understood when you're losing a child.

I anxiously whiled away the hours until I'd be taken to the NICU, the neonatal intensive care unit, to see her. The surprise was that the person pushing the wheelchair into my room, smiling as if everything were perfectly normal, was my mother. 'Did you see her?' is all I asked. 'Yes', she replied. 'I saw her, and she's very pretty.'

My mother rolled my wheelchair down the hall. Along the way, it didn't seem to cross her mind that she could talk to me, offer any details that might prepare me for what I was about to see. It was a silent ride. I hadn't expected my mother. Things can always get worse, I thought.

I remembered a moment from the movie *Bitter Moon* in which Oscar recalls a conversation with his partner Mimi: 'She said, there's bad news and there's good news. You're paralysed from the waist down – permanently. OK, I said, let's have the good news. That *was* the good news, she said. The bad news is that from now on, I'm taking care of you.'

———

When I entered the NICU, a nurse gave my shoulder a gentle squeeze and gestured to the incubator in the middle of the room. A fierce purple light shone down.

Everything was silent, except for the noises that – I now know – constantly report the vital signs of all the babies pulsing there.

———

When they led me to the incubator, I looked and couldn't find her.

I looked again in that rectangular space, small and glassed-over, and there she was.

That was her, MyChild.

That thing.

I fainted.

Her head wasn't much larger than a Christmas bauble. Her body, not much longer than a remote control.

Now, back in my room, reading the reports they gave me, I know that her femur, the longest bone in the human body, is four and a half centimetres long. I use my index finger and thumb to simulate the measurement in the air, trying to fill the space by imagining familiar vertebrates. A chicken's must be larger, I think. It hurts me, the size of her femur. Her bones hurt me.

I return to what one of the doctors said: that micro-preemies are unknown creatures, each is utterly unique, no single formula applies in the attempt to save them all. What's more, MyChild even looks physically unfamiliar to me. Her whole body is covered with lanugo, the fine hair that covers foetuses during pregnancy to protect them from infection and conserve heat, since they're not yet insulated by subcutaneous fat. Normally this hair falls out and is reabsorbed by the amniotic fluid before birth, but my daughter still has hers. Her skin is very wrinkled, as if she'd spent hours in the water, or as if she were ancient – no: the analogies falter as I write this. It's a different kind of wrinkliness I can't make sense of. When I saw her, and now as well, she's halfway between everything. Hair and baldness. The first light and the last. Celebration and grief. The human foetus and the simian one.

I remember another description from the book whose final pages were interrupted by her arrival. I search for the quote. Everything makes sense and nothing does; she's a new animal or an old one. Her animal self contains some kind of natural logic – in her human self, though, I can't find it.

> I knew little about octopuses . . . But what I did know intrigued me. Here is an animal that has venom like a snake, a beak like a parrot, and ink like an old-fashioned pen. It can weigh as much as a man and stretch as long as a car, yet can pour its baggy, boneless body through an opening the size of an orange. It can change colour and shape. It can taste with its skin. Most fascinating of all, I had read that octopuses are smart. This bore out what scant experience I had already had; like many who visit octopuses in public aquaria, I've often had the feeling the octopus I was watching was watching me back, with an interest as keen as my own.

And I think: maybe preemies aren't human. Maybe they're a species that usually dies when they exit the vaginal opening that dilates to the size of an orange. Maybe my daughter has completed a shorter life cycle, like a butterfly or a day-flower. Maybe I shouldn't be sad because she's already lived and now she's old, even if the doctors can't see it and even I can't believe it. Maybe she's watching us somehow, in her incubator, wondering why we've put her there. But no, I know my daughter is human, and she's simply doing something that all species do: dying too soon.

You're as small as the doctor's latex glove. So very small that I have to squint to distinguish your features. Six hundred and fifty-two grams. The limit of viability. You really are half-finished. Your translucent skin reveals blood vessels as delicate as stems of red coral. Your eyes are closed – not just closed, but sealed by a fine membrane. There's a bruise on your forehead, as if you'd taken a spill. The atmosphere is warm and damp, and the walls of the incubator are riddled with tiny bubbles that are born and die, are born and die, and prove that you, MyChild, are breathing. A mask covers your mouth and nose, and there's a sort of bandage around your neck, and I can't figure out where your oxygen tube goes in: your mouth, your nose, your trachea? 'She's intubated,' they tell me, but I still don't understand. I don't understand you, your body, I don't understand it. Your ears aren't shaped like ears and they're stuck to your head. Several heart-shaped electrodes are fastened to your skin. I look at one of your hands: it's barely larger than my thumbnail. You're very thin, your skin is too big for your bones, I can count your breaths by the harried shifting of your ribs, which look like the hull of a miniature boat. At this gestational stage, the doctors repeat, the lack of fat leaves you more vulnerable to infection. Your head, tiny as it is, is disproportionately large for the rest of your body, which still corresponds more to a foetus than to a baby. Several panels shine that purple light onto you; they're supposed to help your liver eliminate bilirubin. An IV in your hand – another small bruise – provides you with nutrients. In a few weeks, if you evolve properly, the IV will be swapped for a nasogastric tube from your nose to your stomach. Now, though, your stomach can't be fed this way. A shipwreck victim with twenty-five weeks at sea, your diminutive guts can't bear the weight of food. You also have a red light fixed on one foot with a bandage; an oximeter, I learn. Your skin is so delicate that the light practically passes through your foot – and still shines brightly enough to glow on the incubator's glass wall. Light itself seems to have more substance, more heft, than your flesh. I'm reminded of E.T.'s finger. My flat. MyChild, our home right now is as far away as an unknown planet. I wish I could swaddle and tuck you into my bicycle basket, ride straight over this hospital, sail all the way home and show you the room I got ready for you. I'm sorry, I mean the room that's still ready for you. Forgive me. Forgive me. You're so small the past tense doesn't mean I'm talking about you as if you don't exist; it's just that the length of your tiny bones will be a thing of the past. This incubator will be like a time machine that will have to transport you to the present, to your baby-size. 'What's this other tube?' I ask the doctor. 'What about that one? Are you sure it isn't too tight?' The nurses explain everything about the machinery, the electrodes, the tape, the little straps, the miniature garments that clothe you. The orography of your minuscule body: a continent of flesh and blood that hasn't yet appeared on any map.

I start taking photos. Of what? I don't know. Your nappy, no longer than a coaster, covers you up to the chest. What am I capturing? A scrap of my body, that's still what it is, it's me, you're me on the worst day of my life, you're me dying, and yes, I take pictures almost reflexively. They're selfies, I think. Selfies I'm stealing from myself without your permission.

You visibly struggle to breathe. The nurse inserts a tube slightly thicker than the lead of a pencil into your trachea. She uses a syringe to administer a white liquid through the tube. It's surfactant bound for your lungs. The same surfactant that, not too many years ago, was extracted from the lungs of animals in slaughterhouses.

I linger beside you after the photos, who knows for how long. I study every movement of your fingers, fine as the stalks of a carnation, skin like a petal pierced by sunlight, mottled with tiny speckles of dewy moisture. You're a delicate ecosystem that could be thrown out of balance at any moment. I stop to take in every one of your features, and it feels as if you're telling me: *Mama, I'm not ready to be alive. Mama, I don't know how to dawn.*

I never read any pregnancy books or took any prenatal classes, because I thought I'd be able to understand you through instinct and age-old knowledge. I know it's not as easy as that, not even with a baby born to term. But what I didn't know is that a preemie is almost entirely incomprehensible. There's nothing in my body that can teach me how to interpret you. There's no maternal dictionary inside me, just hundreds of loose papers spattered with hieroglyphics. Whenever I've held a baby in my arms, I've always felt a basic level of communication, no matter how limited: a yawn is a yawn, a burp is a burp, a sigh is a sigh. With you, any one of those things can mean scores of others, some positive, others not. Not even doctors can decipher whether a smile-like gesture is neutral or indicates some unknown pain. I can't understand you, but it does comfort me to know that no mother in this place can understand their baby: each one speaks their own unique language, utterly distinct from the rest. It seems there's no such thing as premature babies in general, just *a* premature baby, living a wholly different kind of life from that of every other – and so on and so forth with every infant born before term all over the world. Thousands and thousands of species whose mothers are dying to understand them before they go extinct.

But maybe there is a way I can understand MyChild. It comes to mind when I remember a dinner with friends a couple of months back. One of my friends, twenty-three weeks pregnant, had bought an intravaginal device that allows future mothers to play music right into the uterus. This form of stimulation can be used starting in the fourth month of gestation, when a foetus's sense of hearing is considered sufficiently developed. My friend said she'd diligently incorporated this ritual into her pregnancy routine, which otherwise consisted of eight hundred grams of folic acid, refraining from cleaning her cat's litter box (a precaution against toxoplasmosis), getting enough rest, and various other precepts that seemed designed to protect the foetus from the mother. In any case, my friend explained that she lay down in bed every afternoon, chose a piece of classical music, and inserted the little speaker like a tampon or a vibrator.

With great curiosity and maybe a dash of intuition, I said I hadn't realised she liked classical music. She actually didn't like it at all, my friend replied, but she'd always wished she could play an instrument and wanted to foster her child's talent for something she hadn't acquired herself – perhaps because this instrument of prenatal education hadn't been invented yet.

MyChild is statistically unlikely to be a musical genius. In fact, given her premature birth, she may not even develop her full auditory capacity. What I mean, though, is that maybe I can communicate with her more directly through my own emotional responses to a song than by making her listen to it. Maybe she, a tiny being who should still be inside me, will enjoy some kind of sensorial communication: pleasant internal emotions expressed through her mother. After all, according to what the doctors have said, her body hasn't yet registered that she's outside me in the first place. My brain hasn't, either. We're still one and the same. Each of us is the other's phantom limb. I drink a glass of cool water that briefly soothes the tightness in my throat, and I feel like it soothes her too. Studies show that octopuses are capable of perceiving light, and maybe colour, through their skin. MyChild's skin, exposed to the elements, looks as frail as rice paper. Her eyes are still shut, but who can say that she's incapable of sensing my presence in the shadows, my silhouette blocking the light.

Today, the first nurse I met – I have yet to learn their names – opened the lid of the incubator and asked if I wanted to touch you. Her question caught me completely off guard. I didn't answer right away. Isn't it too soon? I thought. She took my hands, carefully disinfected them, and told me to stroke you with light, tiny taps; a normal caress could detach your skin. I don't think I said a single word the entire time. I was afraid, but I placed a finger right onto your skin, applying no pressure. I could make out the perfect shape of your heart, the minuscule muscle pumping away atop the rest of your body. In the centre, my finger. Then I stroked your head, slightly oval-shaped and a bit slippery, and remembered a line from Sy Montgomery's book: 'The bliss of stroking an octopus's head is difficult to convey to most people, even to animal lovers.' I'd say the same about stroking a preemie's head: no one can come close to imagining this joy.

What's left of your life seems so fragile that I don't dare move when I'm with you. I don't want the noise of my footsteps to interrupt your breathing – which, in certain fleeting moments, sounds like a steady whistle that would correspond to an E if played on an instrument. In the morning, I prepare everything I need to spend the rest of the day in this chair, right across from you: my one-string violin. In your present state, I'm not sure if your body heeds any cycles of wakefulness and sleep. The sound persists at night, although it's no longer a violin. It's a piano with one key.

And then there's what I don't see: your brain. What the doctors fear the most. The human brain, the layer that distinguishes us from other animals, is the final organ a baby develops. Will it finish developing out in the open, beyond the mother's evacuated body? Sometimes, yes. Most times, no. I find myself thinking of a neighbour. He's eighteen and has severe cerebral palsy. Every day, his parents – always both of them – take him out for a walk in his wheelchair. The first few times I saw him, I instinctively looked away, until one day I didn't. Later, on another day when we found ourselves seated at nearby tables on the patio of a restaurant, I asked his name. Of course, I knew he wasn't going to answer, but his parents replied for him; they were proud to do so, proud to have their son respond to someone who dared look at and even greet him. That's what they said: everyone averts their eyes, avoids striking up a conversation. Their son Diego appreciates not only the smattering of words that the occasional person offers forth, but also their touch. Since then, whenever I see them, I hug Diego and ask him questions for his parents to answer as he smiles.

I don't want people to look away when you pass by. According to the doctors, though, the chances are high. Best not get ahead of ourselves. They explain that the brain of a baby born at twenty-five weeks is still in a very early developmental phase. At this gestational age, the brain continues to rapidly grow and mature. It remains extremely small, fragile and susceptible to damage. Even the slightest lack of oxygen or any kind of bleeding (a dreaded outcome for a preemie) can be fatal. The brain has its characteristic gyri and folds, but they haven't evolved like those of a baby born to term, and you can't see them. The doctors show me an image of your brain: it looks like a chicken on a supermarket tray, slick and featherless and totally smooth. I flinch as if it were about to attack me.

I've always fallen in love with men for their intelligence, and here I am now, mother of a child who may never come to speak. But YourMother will speak for you. And YourMother will be overjoyed if you survive. And Mama will answer when anyone asks your name.

Once I started paying attention to baby clothes, I developed a distaste for dinosaurs. Previously, these extinct animals were part of an imaginary group I willingly entered and exited whenever I saw the near-perfect fossil of the *Tyrannosaurus rex* at the Museum of Natural History in New York, or the *Diplodocus* skeleton at the Naturhistorisches Museum in Vienna. The occasional childhood memory would bring me back; when I was little, all my cousins wanted to do was play with dinosaurs. I'd outgrown the thrill by then, but I didn't mind playing along for a while.

When I got pregnant, my life suddenly filled with dinosaurs again. They're everywhere: baby clothes, children's clothes, and far from being extinct in the realm of toys, they've multiplied into millions of plastic figurines. A few months ago, someone gave me a dinosaur mobile to hang over your cot. I bought one with present-day animals instead: elephants, giraffes, monkeys, tigers. I'd rather mimic the sounds of animals you'll be able, hopefully, to hear one day. Who knows what sounds dinosaurs made. And how would their unpronounceable names help you learn your first words? Meanwhile, especially in my scarce moments of relative optimism, I try to believe that the future exists. I long to show you the parts of the world still accessible to us; to reveal the fauna we can still see, still touch with our eyes. Animals that still exist in spite of us, bound to our environment, revelling in a world I can't wait to share with you. Even so, the childhood – and childish – market insists on dinosaurs, dinosaurs, dinosaurs everywhere. A bona fide invasion.

Today, a nurse told me I could place a toy on top of the incubator, and so I found myself thinking about the mobile: giraffes, elephants, tigers, monkeys. Then my heart took a terrible plunge. What if, in my specific circumstances, in my state of unfortunate exception, dinosaurs make more sense? Dr Truong told me that your brain is still very smooth; it hasn't finished developing the part of this mammalian organ that defines us as humans and determines functions like language and memory. I think you must still have a reptilian brain, an almost entirely reactive organ controlling unconscious functions: your heartbeat, your breath. Your muscles too, if barely. But you do respond: when they inject you with something or draw your blood, your hands contract, your forehead creases. You react like a lizard or a crocodile.

I want to think of you as human now. Someday you'll be ready for me to tell you what an elephant is, and how the dinosaurs went extinct, and how we don't have to pay them any mind, because we too once found ourselves on the verge of extinction and those are days we'd rather forget.

No truces here. The doctors need to make sure I'm fully informed of everything that could happen to you. They explain that at this early stage, your brain cells, your neurons, are rapidly proliferating and connecting to each other and can't be interrupted. Your neural pathways are also forming: the communication circuits that enable electrical and chemical signals to be transmitted in the brain. All of this is essential for a person to seem like a person. That's not how they put it, but it's what they mean.

Present pain is always worse than past pain. It's younger, still growing. My pain has teenage bones, and they're stretching. I prefer uncertainty. I start to seek refuge in doubt. Sometimes doubt hurts less than hope. But I look at you and everything turns to certainty. Your weight in grams is a certainty. Your low temperature is a certainty. The thermometer or oximeter seem like gauges of death.

Sometimes I'm furious. Everything in this hospital – in all hospitals, but I'd never noticed before now – is designed to distinguish medical professionals from patients. This distinction expresses itself in every possible way. While doctors and nurses glide freely down the halls, patients are confined to their rooms. Besides, the latter are the ones receiving orders, often rudely. They're more like prisoners inside a prison inside another prison: illness inside the hospital. In your case, this confinement is even more obvious: illness inside an incubator inside a hospital. My head echoes with the words, transmuted now, of Segismundo in Pedro Calderón de la Barca's play *Life Is a Dream*:

What crime did I commit
against you with my birth?
Though I was born indeed, I now discern
the crime I have committed . . .
But were not others also born?
For if they were,
what rights did they enjoy
that I myself have never known?[3]

I contemplate your confinement. What crime have you committed?

Being born.

Only being born.

And now I remember. It's not that I'd forgotten, but my family never spoke of it again. I must have been about six when it happened. It was on another beach. The death of another little girl, my three-year-old cousin. I remember a lot about that day. It was back in Spain, on a beach in Huelva. Inspections were activated on the border with Portugal in case my cousin had been abducted. This might explain some things, but I'm not yet sure. The beach.

When I was pregnant, a friend told me that his mother, who lives in Nigeria, once saw a woman drift away from the group of people she was with and retreat behind some bushes. She re-emerged minutes later with a newborn in her arms. I believed it at the time. Now I'd rather not. Now I'd rather think it's just a racist anecdote insinuating that Black women have a more animalistic experience of childbirth: back on their feet right away, as if time rushed ahead in anticipation of a potential predator, a furtive hunter lying in wait. If I'd gone into labour in the middle of the woods, or on a plane, we both would have died. Once I had a boyfriend who made me crazy because we'd spend entire days in bed and he'd call me a 'female'. I thought it was a terrible word in light of my feminist activism, my politicised master's degrees, my PhD. A terrible word for a human being, especially since he'd accompanied it with the possessive 'my', 'my female', which I found ideologically enraging. But in truth it also made me so wet that whenever he was about to penetrate me, he'd slip out a few times until he succeeded. And it drove him wilder and wilder to find me so wet, and so he'd say it again and again: 'My female.' I wouldn't want him to see me in my current state, stripped of my capacity to give life without dying. I'm not the female animal, the powerful female-woman, who would have given birth all alone if necessary, clutching a tree trunk. Making the species prosper without any need for a team of countless doctors joining forces to resuscitate her. I'm not a female. I'm not strong enough to survive on my own. And yet I still call myself YourMother. You, MyChild, are still alive.

I'd like to think that these lacerating, hormone-fuelled days are filling my head with false and intrusive thoughts. Here are some of them:

My body wasn't capable of properly carrying out its most primitive natural functions: gestation and childbirth.

If it were up to me, *Homo sapiens* would die out on this planet.

Or maybe we wouldn't die out. Maybe, if you and

many other babies like you managed to survive, the outcome would be like something I read about once: the bones of ancient humans were found on an island of Indonesia, measuring no more than a metre long, with heads the size of grapefruits. It turns out that these prehistoric beings reached the island when it was still part of the continent, and when the waters rose, their food ran out. The only survivors were those who could subsist on very few calories, and their children, and their children's children, and the children of their children's children, who started to forge a new species of diminutive *Homo*. And so, if you and other micropreemies could survive, maybe you'd ultimately create a race of humans plugged into cables and machines, with renal failure and bags for evacuating your faeces. Humans stuck to monitors beeping out your vital signs. Just as we're now dragged along in the wake of our employers, who punch in the digits of our economy as we dance to its beat. The labour machine we depend on is a domineering human who oversees the quality of our nutrition, the composition and frequency of our defecations, our leisure time. But at least that machine is smart enough to lie to us, as if it were doing it all for our own good. When I study your machine – MyBaby's machine, right in front of me – it sometimes looks arrogant to me, as if our fate really did hinge on its whims. It doesn't lie to me. It doesn't seem to be doing anything for my own good. Nor to my detriment. You, MyChild, are like a bird in the open palm of a gorilla, which examines you intently. It could crush you or set you free. Its will is arbitrary:

Rock-a-bye baby, on the treetop,
When the wind blows, the cradle will rock,

When the bough breaks, the cradle will fall,
And down will come baby, cradle and all.
(Or not.)

No doctor offers any guarantees, not even with facial expressions that my unfounded hope might interpret as encouraging. These days, I inhabit the radical present of *my daughter's heart is beating right now*, a pound of flesh struggling for breath in a transparent ark, right in plain sight. Months before your due date, the doctors and I, YourMama, can already see your organs, your fingernails, your tiny ears continuing to form. I feel that none of them but me should have the right to witness MyBaby struggling to dress herself this way. Just three days ago, in the latest ultrasound, they called you 'foetus'. Today they called you 'baby'. Welcome to this world, ChildOfMine. Just three days ago, I might have thought differently, but today I'm asking you: stay, even if your breathing depends on my care for every passing second of your life and mine. It's hard for me to say it, it's even hard to hear myself think it, but please, stay here with me. Even if you feel pain in parts of your body you don't yet have. Even if you someday resent me for having kept you alive. My selfishness is appalling, which is why I have no trouble repeating it over and over:

Stay.
Stay.
Stay.

It's been well studied that reason and feelings aren't two separate boxes we open to take decisions in accordance with our minds or our so-called hearts. Reason and feelings are inextricable when it comes to decision-taking. There's no such thing as thinking with your head or with your heart. In fact, there's an illness – Urbach-Wiethe disease[4] – in which patients have calcifications on the amygdala, the part of the brain that regulates emotions, especially fear. These patients can reason logically with no trouble at all, but they're unable to decide anything. I asked the doctors to try and save your life no matter what, no matter the cost, no matter how terrible the side effects. Contrary to appearances, this was a decision taken by both organs, brain and heart. Which makes me feel a bit less guilty. And the possible side effects won't be caused by my feelings or impulses at a specific moment; they'll also be the result of my reflections, because that's how it always is, that's how decisions are taken. That's how it works for us humans.

Every passing day means a tiny increase in your chances of getting out of here alive. But today is day six, and I can't stop thinking about it: we're still trapped in an ominous limbo with a tragically sweet name, the honeymoon phase. The time when micropreemies seem like miracles of strength, and then are gone.

The Neonatal Intensive Care Unit is on the fourth floor of the hospital. It's important for me to get to know it, I'm told. They guide me, they show me around.

Inside, I find a large white hall lit by glacier-coloured fluorescent tubes, opening out before me like a sanctuary. A choir of frail, mechanised breathing allures and repels me at once. The intense aurora borealis glow is mitigated by the walls and the floor, which are covered with an opaque, resistant, easy-to-clean material to protect occupants from infection.

An entire wall is outfitted with an enormous control panel: the master key that supervises every heartbeat in the place. From there, specialists monitor the electronic equipment and panels that register the infants' vital signs.

In the middle of the hall, several stainless-steel worktables gleam with reflected light. Each table is laid with precision instruments, as well as a computer showing the micropatients' graphics and statistics. The medical personnel sit on ergonomic plastic chairs, their movements both alert and still. Like lurking predators: backs arched, chests close to the ground, motionless but ready to pounce.

They warn me not to touch or open anything. Everything in this place has a function that could fail if contaminated by an inexpert hand. The stainless-steel cabinets contain sterilised medical supplies. One corner of the hall is devoted to an antiseptic soap dispenser: a vital fluid against infection. It's one of those automatic devices that releases the proper quantity of soap when it detects the presence of a hand below, but it's larger, more imposing than the ones I'm used to seeing. Beside it is a paper towel dispenser.

The hand-washing station is the best-lit corner in the room, equipped with several sinks so several people can disinfect themselves at once. The electronic taps control the water's temperature and duration.

In another corner is the wardrobe station for the medical staff, equipped with lockers and hangers to store their clothes and personal belongings. I notice an open locker, observe everything inside it, and wonder if the owner abandoned it in the middle of an emergency, because, unlike everything else, it's messy. The door to the small waiting room for patients' families is always open.

All of this exists to sustain and nurture the main part, the living centre of this place: the incubators and preemies. These are located in a calm adjacent area. Although 'calm' isn't an entirely positive thing. We might say that the hall is designed to soothe these miniature lives, but when tranquillity drifts into silence, the nurses' demeanour darkens. That's how one of them puts it to me: 'Silence is never good news in here.' Since my first glimpse of these babies' fatless bodies, I've understood the fear of any kind of thinning-down, even of sound.

The incubators are arranged in orderly lines. God forgive me (god, lowercase? what god?), but they look like the sarcophagi of fallen soldiers, their disposition so strict it makes me shiver. I imagine a flag draped over each incubator, the flags of many nations, the slain children of sundry lands, some so far-flung that their mothers can't be here.

A translucent curtain can be drawn to separate an incubator from the other patients when privacy is required, or when a high-stakes medical procedure begins. Or when a child dies. In any case, a curtain is never a good sign. Everything seems to follow an order here: if a baby dies, then it feels like the next person to walk out alone will be the mother nearest the curtain. I'm an organised person, yet all this organisation feels like rolling out the red carpet for tragedy to strike. If it were up to me, I'd rearrange everything, invite a kind of chaos that would make this hall look more like the world we breathe out there.

Dr Truong seems to be the most relevant actor in my daughter's care. He's of Korean descent, tall, with a warm and welcoming air, though I've never seen him smile. His hair is dark and thick, combed back and neatly gelled, which makes him too meticulous for my liking, as if he had too much time on his hands. He's an impeccable dresser too; under his white lab coat, a pastel buttoned shirt and necktie add a touch of elegance to his outfit, which, once again, feels too fastidious for the circumstances. His shoes are black and polished, but at least they look comfortable.

Today Dr Truong has good news and bad news. The good news is that premature girls tend to be more resilient than boys. The bad news is I'm not Black, because African-American girls have higher rates of survival. Once again, I'd like to believe that this is a myth as racist as the bit about African women who give birth alone and are back on their feet within minutes. But this one isn't a myth, it's science. Facts. Statistics.

The nurses are always repeating that if preemies manage to take one step forwards, they then take two steps back. That's how it works. Apparently, no preemies take more forwards steps than back. But I look at you and wonder how you'll survive so much as a single backwards step. It's like looking at a tadpole and thinking it'll have to devolve into some prior state – a phase underwent even before it became a tadpole – before it can ever fully morph into a frog. This reminds me of something I wrote while researching the side effects of radiation on women's bodies after the atomic bombing of Hiroshima. Listen, MyChild. The image pierced me. A pregnant woman. Her belly. Instead of growing, it began to shrink in the sixth month. As if it had changed its mind, her belly retraced its steps, foetus to sperm, seeking its former flatness, before gestation.

A nurse I'm meeting for the first time, or at least I think so, comes over to tell me about your incubator. It's the Giraffe Incubator Carestation: one of the most widely used, most advanced models in the so-called first world. She says it's a closed incubator, designed for babies that need the highest possible degree of protection, maximum isolation from external germs, strict control over light and sound and an exhaustive register of temperature and humidity. It's the closest thing to an artificial atmosphere on a planet that has suddenly expelled me, shot me into the air through a crack in its crystal dome. And now I'm floating in orbit, watching you construct yourself without the help of my hands. I'm an architect who left a house half-built, and now the roof is caving in. All this rubble – where is my daughter?

I study the incubator intently as the nurse continues to praise the machine, and I'm grateful, but it also feels like she's trying to sell it to me:

An adjustable bed that elevates and inclines for easier access to the baby, or to keep her in the proper position for breathing. This also lets mums recovering from childbirth adjust the height of the incubator and see their baby without hurting themselves.

High-quality materials on the side walls for easy viewing of the baby.

A heated mattress that keeps the baby at the proper temperature without blankets or any other accessories that might smother her.

The baby's temperature is controlled automatically through an integrated sensor. This sensor also adjusts the thermal cot to keep the baby within the proper range and guarantee her safety and comfort: between thirty-six point five and thirty-seven point five degrees Celsius.

A touch screen allows doctors and nurses to precisely and (if necessary) manually adjust the temperature, humidity and other important parameters.

A filter system keeps the air inside the incubator clean and free of contaminants, which is essential to preventing infection.

A sensor gauges the quantity of oxygen inside the incubator and provides medical personnel with key information to ensure that the baby receives the correct amount.

The nurse motions to the screen above the incubator: it shows the baby's heart and respiratory rates, blood pressure and oxygen saturation levels.

A respiratory support system with mechanical ventilation and CPAP functions helps the baby breathe in case of respiratory problems.

Adjustable LED illumination system. Ports and entrances allow access to the baby for medical procedures, such as the administration of medications and the drawing of blood. I freeze at this last phrase. Blood? They're going to draw blood? How much? The blood circulating through MyChild's body would fill a pair of spoons.

The colour of my daughter's blood is startling to me: it's red. This makes her seem more human. Iron, haemoglobin, transports her oxygen. An octopus's blood is blue because copper does so, not iron. Iron unites us. Maybe we've reached the final age of metals:

Copper Age (ca. 5000 BCE).

Bronze Age (ca. 3000 BCE).

Iron Age (ca. 1200 BCE).

Are we there? Does this mean that the next step is to enter the Age of History, and of your existence in that history, which begins with writing? I know it's not true; writing to you serves no purpose. But I still want to believe that writing to you means I'm making you, delivering you from distant eras into the present. Writing to you means locating you in history, tracing your silhouette in the mist your breath leaves on the mirror. So, what happened in the story of the other beach, the one where my cousin died? A story silenced, quelled by my family's pain and guilt. Where did my cousin die and when did we stop talking about it? In the Copper Age? Was it that her blood was blue? Why was my cousin essentially blotted from my family history?

Many years ago, just after I moved to New York, someone knocked on my door. When I opened it, I found myself facing an enormous man in a Ghostbusters suit who introduced himself like this: 'I'm the exterminator.' I barely spoke any English and felt my blood run cold, but one of my roommates invited him in as if it were the most natural thing in the world. When the exterminator left, she explained that he stopped by every couple of weeks to control pests, from cockroaches to rats. My mother was visiting at the time – not to see me, but to take in the Empire State Building, Broadway musicals, the lights of Times Square, the usual attractions.

In any case, while reading in my flat a few days later, I heard a clicking sound behind the sofa. When I peeked over, I saw a mouse caught in a trap, its neck broken and the lower part of its body still convulsing. I hadn't expected that. I didn't enjoy the surprise or yet know how many others awaited me all around the house. Days later, I was cooking when I saw another mouse by the fridge, alive this time, snared in a glue trap. When my mother caught me unsticking its tiny paws with her pure acetone nail polish remover, she said that was the last time I'd be using her beauty products. I kept at it for an hour until the mouse broke free. It was either that or throwing it into the rubbish, still alive. Or worse, finding it as I'd come to find other mice: dragging itself along, trailing blood, after it had gnawed off its own limbs in the attempt to escape.

I saved an ordinary mouse that day. And I've saved many creatures over the course of my life. But of all of them it's you – your life pulsing in the incubator, your body I caress as often as I can – that's the most helpless animal I've ever seen. More than the kitten whose belly was swollen with worms. More than the lamb I ran off with as a child, hoping in vain to spare it from slaughter; it did get its throat cut in the end. More than the puppy my grandfather and I rescued from between the tyres of a truck and which survived to become my childhood pet, although she only had three legs.

You don't seem to be dying. But you don't seem to be living, either. It's more like you're dying *out*. Dying is easy, dying out is difficult. I've been witnessing what's most difficult. An animal that's dying out is still alive, and yet it also means a radical death: its passing contains the end of its entire species. You're like one of the two last white rhinoceroses left in the world, mother and daughter. I wish I could protect you inside the incubator. I wonder why they haven't invented incubators with room for mothers, and I know my question wouldn't make sense even if they had. But the threads of my thinking take irrational turns: couldn't they have left you connected to me through the umbilical cord, then placed both of us inside this glass urn? That way I could have kept feeding you as you're supposed to be fed, and we'd stay together. I'd keep you warm, we'd keep communicating through physical contact. Then all this glass would be the uterus, but I'd still be able to fulfil the placenta's vital functions. Now, though, what purpose do I have? Just six days ago, you couldn't survive without me. Today you can. Can't you?

Every two hours, I watch the nurses carry out their vital routine:

They lift the lid of the incubator, exposing the miniature world within.

They change your nappy with utmost care, place it on a tray for fluid analysis.

They take your temperature. Any variation warrants monitoring every twenty minutes.

They check the fit of your oxygen mask to ensure it's properly positioned, adequately sealed to provide the respiratory support you need. They meticulously adjust the bands to guarantee both effectiveness and comfort.

They scrutinise every centimetre of your skin in search of tears, sores, abrasions.

They change your position so that the plates of your skull, not yet fused shut, won't warp or flatten. The material of your head is still as malleable as damp clay.

Finally, they extract a sample from the contents of your stomach for analysis. They draw it through your feeding tube with a syringe. Depending on the results, they adjust your nutrition.

In this hall, some mothers hold their babies in their arms just once: to give them heat, form, love, as they die. And they stay like that for hours, cradling their babies who no longer breathe. They talk and sing, they promise to always be there, to never forget them, they tell the baby stories about their families, about their pets, describe the special room they'd prepared, their cot, their pyjamas, their stuffed animals. And I know these mothers will go home and want to die. But in those moments, all I see is a mother who loves her daughter, her son, and takes care of them and sings to them like any other mother on earth. If I didn't know any better, I'd think the baby was a healthy baby. I don't see the sorrow, the despair, the suicidal thoughts lurking in the empty hall. It's a beautiful and terrible moment because it's real. And in that moment, in that very moment, the dead children are alive.

One of the nurses told me that when she started working with micropreemies, only those born weighing over a thousand grams were counted as deceased. The others – the babies who weighed eight hundred grams, or nine hundred and fifty grams, even if they lived for days – were documented as miscarriages. In the best-case scenario, some nurses, furtively and with the parents' consent, offered to place the tiny baby in an adult-sized coffin, which meant they'd receive a burial and some form of companionship. If this thousand-gram limit still applied today, some of us in this hospital wouldn't even have the right to a death certificate. I'd never granted any positive significance to those certificates until now. They always have a mournful air – unless it's important, crucial, utterly necessary to know and let others know that your daughter was here in the world, that she was born alive, that she breathed, ate, fought, gave it her all. This can't be a miscarriage.

My cousin is buried in a cemetery in Seville. My Aunt Carmen, who has since returned to grow old there, now evokes her more than ever. In truth, I don't think what I've just written is true; I doubt she's gone a single day without thinking of her daughter. All I mean is that she's recently started to name her, to share certain specific details after each visit to her grave. I've gained a greater appreciation of how important it is to have the flesh of your flesh contained somewhere, in a familiar place. Even if it's where you scattered the ashes into the air, where you too can rest. In the mercilessness of tragedy, at least there's a breeze that soothed my aunt: my cousin's body was found. The significance of a burial exceeds the magnitude of oblivion. At the same time, it lets you treasure your memories instead of trapping yourself among the rocks like a blind fish, searching in vain for a way out.

For the Church to define something as a miracle, it must be scientifically inexplicable.

Five years ago, a woman underwent an emergency C-section in a San Diego hospital. The mother begged the doctors to wait: 'She's only twenty-three weeks, she won't make it.' But without a C-section, both mother and daughter would die. That's how the world's smallest baby was born. Her weight: two hundred and forty-five grams, as much as an apple. The doctors told the mother that her baby wouldn't live more than an hour. That hour stretched into more hours, days, weeks, and then to five months, when she was discharged in good health. When the mother asked one of the nurses how the baby could have possibly survived, the nurse responded, 'It's a miracle. I swear.' What I'm about to say contradicts my agnosticism, but I don't think a woman can walk out of here with her baby alive and not profoundly believe in miracles. Every new day that dawns with my living daughter in it, my faith becomes more tangible. It's not a blind faith; it's the faith of someone who can and wants to touch the wound. Some might say that this isn't faith at all. Who cares – it's still a miracle. Or maybe, in the words of Sy Montgomery, 'Once you find the right way to work with an animal, be it an octopus or an anaconda, together, you can accomplish what even Saint Francis might have considered a miracle.' Maybe the miracle is the symbiosis between the cells that want to live and the cells that help them.

Day seven. I won't be able to hold her in my arms just yet: today she's struggling harder to breathe and they've fitted her with a high-frequency, more invasive ventilator, which applies constant pressure to keep her alveoli open. But they also inserted a horrible tube into her mouth, a 'tracheal tube' – as if the technical term made it any less horrible – that produces powerful bursts of air with violent vibrations. MyBaby vibrates so hard that her whole body shakes, all the time. That's the worst part: it's like she's lying on top of a washing machine on a spin cycle. The noise upsets me too. They've sedated her slightly so she won't get stressed. She's visibly drowsier, though I'm not sure if it's because of the medication or because her condition is worsening. Is this the last day of her honeymoon phase? For now, I don't dare ask. I can't ask everything I think, I can't ask what makes sense and what doesn't, I can't ask about the truth or about my ghosts, or else I'd never stop asking – I'd ask, ask, ask until I turned back into a little girl who's always asking why this and why that, turning to her non-parents, interrogating adults who don't have time to respond, who often wouldn't know what to say even if they did. And I'd become a burden for MyChild, working against the attention and care that must be devoted to her survival without the distractions of a mother who can't stop asking questions that no one can answer. So I keep silent most of the time.

Today I've taken to smiling at the doctors and nurses. I laugh at myself. I'm pathetic. Hopefully I'll be able to tell you this someday and we'll have a laugh together. I'm acting like an idiot. I hope they can't tell. What I really want is for them to like me and pay you more attention than the other babies. It's not easy, because there's a doctor for practically every part of your body – so many doctors, so much putting on appearances for them (which has never been my forte). I smile for no reason. I smile so that, if a baby has to die, it'll be another woman's and not mine, because my pleasantness and charm will have made you the staff favourite. So I ask if there's anything I can do to help, and I bring them coffee on the night shift, and I show interest in their families, which I couldn't care less about, but I memorise the names and hobbies of your caretakers' children – so I can ask after them, so they'll like you best, so they'll save us by force of sheer favouritism.

That said, I never manage to remember the name of Katy's parrot. Katy is the night nurse. I ask about it and she tells me: on her hardest days, when she gets home, the parrot perches on her shoulder and it brings her peace. She's sure that the parrot is capable of empathy. And I, forgetting its name (and unable to ask again or she'll see that I really don't care), can't decide if it's best to ask generically, 'How's your parrot?' or just shut up and ask about absolutely anything other than her stupid bird.

It's one of my earliest memories: I plucked a cockatiel we had at home, stripped it feather by feather. My mother told me off, but she hugged and kissed me too. She was still kind then. Much later, when I was eleven or twelve, my mother and I went out in a small boat to fish for octopuses. The first thing she told me, and the first thing I confirmed on the first day, was that octopuses find ways to disappear as soon as they're let loose on deck. No matter how tiny the hole, even one small as a coin, a large octopus can fit inside it. My mother had become elusive by then. I tried to keep her close by getting good marks, by being sweet and affectionate, anything I could think of, but she'd always slip away into openings I couldn't see. She'd just vanish. Now, as I look at MyChild, I find her so different from every other baby that I wish my brain were more flexible, more octopus-like, to help me understand her. And maybe my mother too.

Sometimes it's like a premonition. I sense that we've been given some time, but I don't know how much. In any case, very little. How does death succeed in trickling through the cracks of a time beyond its dominion, seeping into pores that haven't yet opened? Like in an old song my mother used to sing, I look around and check the doors to make sure death can't creep in: I shut them, seal the windows, shield your incubator. I beg for more time. At least five years, I think absurdly, please give me five years with her, though why ask for five instead of fifty? And in those moments when it seems like you're on your way out, I look at you and plead for a day, just one, and who knows why I ask for a day and not five years. I hear the song's rejoinder in my head: *Un día no puedo darte, una hora tiene de vida / I cannot offer you a day, an hour of life is all there is.*

Once again, I check the doors, windows, incubator, so no one can get in; I block the entrance to the white-clad nurse who isn't a nurse, but someone who's come to take MyChild away. I want to recover the umbilical cord that once united us. I weave something with my own hands: it's not the cord, although I wish it were, but a fantasy, nonsense, a mind game to keep myself from shattering the window and throwing myself out, clearing the way for you. I cling to this ancestral symbol, desperate to perpetuate the bond, the cord, the cord, if I live you live, if I live you live. I fantasise about knotting threads of flesh, cords of arteries, that slip between my fingers, the cord, the cord extending all the way into your incubator and fastening to your belly and coiling like a snake that pumps my life, my own life towards you, as it did before.

I cannot offer you a day, an hour of life is all there is.

Alarms.

Cardiac arrest.

The army of doctors storms in.

It's 4:03 in the morning.

I knew it.

I've lived in New York for over twenty years. Before the arrival of my mother, your grandmother, I spent the last month of my pregnancy cooking, so I'd have enough frozen food on hand and she wouldn't have to lift a finger once you were born. I didn't want my mother to clean or help me with housework; I didn't need any of those things that other mothers naturally offer when their daughters have just given birth. All I wanted was her to hold and soothe you, her granddaughter, for the few days she'd be spending here before flying back to Spain. I wanted her to sing to you, make time to love you. Before her trip, she promised with her usual immaturity or fancifulness to take good care of me. 'I don't need you to take care of me,' I said. 'I only want you to pamper MyBaby.' And in hopes of changing the subject, I told her what I was cooking, phone pressed between my ear and shoulder – a foot and a half from the cooking pots, because my belly was in the way between my once-flat abdomen and the stove.

Besides cooking, and mostly for my mother's sake, I got the house ready. I nested for you, but also for your grandmother. It's hard to explain how ridiculous it felt, the need for motherly approval at a time when you're supposed to be single-mindedly focused on preparing for your child. I thought my own transition into motherhood would release me from my abandoned-puppy grievances, but no. In furnishing your bedroom, I was also arranging it for my mother's eyes: a cot, the sheets, the paintings on the walls. It's a small flat, so I sold the elliptical machine I'd intended to use for postpartum exercise, replacing it with a new bed so my mother could sleep comfortably while you slept with me in my room. I didn't want to bother her. I also bought a bedside table and placed it beside her bed, and I set it with a framed photograph of us. I must be about three years old in the photo. My mother holds me in her arms on the deck of the ferry that's taking us to the Canary Islands, where we spent my first few years; my father's work required frequent moves. My mother – beautiful, incredibly elegant – stands in profile and motions to the ocean as I clutch her neck, looking frightened. I put the photo there for her; she liked it. But she complained about the size of the bedside table: 'I don't know where to put my things.' That was one of her first protestations. At the same time, she sent photos to her friends that showed 'how nicely I'd prepared everything' – not to praise me, but to show them that she deserved no less.

My great-grandmother Dolores used to call 'albóndigas' (meatballs) 'almóndigas', and my little cousin and I would snicker at her mispronunciation. Today, the alternate spelling is considered correct, although it's all the same to me; I don't need a dictionary to authorise the bold, fickle life of words. I'm not sure why, but the word 'almóndigas' brings me back to the days when my grandfather would appear in the kitchen of the country house, which always smelled of woodsmoke, and all of us cousins could instantly tell what he'd done: one of the property's countless feral cats had given birth again and my grandfather had done away with the kittens. I don't know how we knew, because the adults hid it from us, but we knew, just as we knew that my grandfather did it before the kittens had opened their eyes and that this somehow absolved him of the deed. As if opening one's eyes had something to do with the onset of life or the ability to feel pain. Sometimes he'd come into the kitchen and say 'Their eyes are open,' which communicated to my cousins and me that the kittens were still alive, and then we'd eagerly ask when we could see them. My aunt Isabel was always the one to show me the hiding place their mother had chosen, but she wouldn't let us touch or pester them. That's how important their open eyes were: a single blink stood between their fate by drowning in a bucket and the chance to keep nursing at their mother's teats, protected by my grandmother's sister, who we called Tita Isabel and had, not that it matters (or maybe it does?), the intellectual capacity of a child. A nearly sixty-year-old child whose intense blue eyes glimmered when we watched cartoons, or when we asked her not to tattle on us if we did something we weren't supposed to. Tita Isabel protected us just like the cats who'd been saved by a blink of their eyes.

Today, your first kitten-cry, your eyes are still closed. They're translucent, and they look like they're covering two tiny almonds.

I remember all of this because almóndigas were one of the dishes I cooked before my mother came.

The ingredients in my great-grandmother Dolores's almóndigas (serving four) were:

Olive oil

400 grams of ground beef

4 large, ripe tomatoes

1 white onion
3 cloves of garlic
1 egg
300 grams of breadcrumbs
A pinch of salt
Thyme to taste
Parsley to taste
A small handful of almonds

With the pandemic, depending on the density of COVID cases at the time, unaccompanied childbirth has become widespread. Women protest having to endure labour without being able to hold their partner's hand, without their own mother. When a new outbreak hits, relatives and friends have to gather in the hospital waiting room – if they're lucky, that is, because sometimes they're relegated to the carpark. People don't only die alone; they give birth alone too. In New York, each hospital has its own rules, and in this one my mother is allowed inside, given the critical, extremely serious circumstances afflicting both you and me.

But the solitude unleashed by the pandemic didn't catch me by surprise, not a bit. In truth, I'd known something about pandemic loneliness for a long time. When I heard grandparents on the news, weeping and lamenting because they had to see their grandchildren on FaceTime or from the other side of a doorway, I found them thoroughly melodramatic. Although maybe all of this is normal, and I'm the abnormal one: a person who doesn't understand – or didn't yet understand – why countless grandmothers all over the world would cry over not being able to hold their grandchildren. Loneliness isolates you not only from the presence of other humans, but also from empathising with them. It means that, when a global quarantine comes crashing down on you, you think *Big deal.* But if you live, MyBaby, I won't be the cause of your isolation. I'd never make you feel that way. To experience the kind of loneliness imposed by a mother, you'd have to undergo another plague, another global quarantine. And not even then would you understand a jot of that forced, even lethal maternal seclusion. In the future, in another pandemic, I'll be one of the women mourning the impossibility of hugging you and your children. In the future, I'll understand and be grateful for that shared sorrow, the sort I haven't yet treated with the respect it deserves.

———

In the countryside where I spent much of my childhood, stories were passed from mouth to ear. Reading was always oral and authors didn't matter, or else they simply lost their way in the forest, threaded between voices, vanishing like echoes. Their subject matter was necessarily brutal. Because a friend of mine drowned in a well. Because I come from the land of Lorca; because Mr and Mrs Lizard are crying over their lost wedding ring (I'll recite his poem to you, I'll sing it for you). Because popular Andalusian Spanish uses diminutives to mitigate spells of drought. Because the year when my little cousin died at the beach was a year of drought so severe that the water was cut off for hours every day. My great-grandmother told me endless stories by candlelight, and as she cooked she'd say, 'Good cooking, like good stories, comes about in the glow of a fire.' And then there was my grandfather Juan, who worked so hard to teach me about all the plants and creatures of the countryside, who taught me to orientate myself, as if he suspected I'd someday end up lost and alone and would have to learn to survive. Although I was already alone back then. And the countryside that taught me to understand and therefore survive no longer exists. Instead I live, we live, in a city that disorientates me more than ever; lost and empty-headed, clutching my brains in my hand, searching for a trash can to dump them in, cars swerving as I lurch robotically across the highway, insulting me: 'Crazy lady! Idiot!'

I won't go out walking unless I can carry you in my arms. If you make it out of here alive, you'll be my lung, my Andalusian meadow, my great Central Park inside our little flat: the lake with its ducks and pedal boats, the squirrels, the hundred-year-old carousel with its beautiful carved, painted wooden horses, the angel-woman of the waters who crowns the Bethesda Fountain. And the children, all the kids who come to play in our home's very own Central Park.

By the way, when I went up to the cafeteria today, I saw a starling perched on a windowsill. I'll tell you this whole story in more detail too: one snowy day in 1890, Eugene Schieffelin freed sixty starlings in Central Park, triggering one of the greatest natural disasters in North America. Now, descending from those sixty starlings and another forty he set loose the following year, there are more than two hundred million. One reason why starlings seem to multiply infinitely is that their beak muscles are unusually powerful, which allows them to open their mouths underground for easier access to invertebrate prey. Schieffelin intended to colonise the United States with all the birds ever mentioned in the works of Shakespeare. But today, when I saw the starling, I saw not a bird but a plague of locusts toothed with your possible annihilation. I glimpsed all of this in sixty seconds' worth of feathers: I saw so many dead children raining down beyond the cafeteria windows that I couldn't count them fast enough. Non-believer though I am, I found myself thinking of John's words in the Book of Revelations:

> ... and the third part of trees was burnt up, and all green grass was burnt up ... and as it were a great mountain burning with fire was cast into the sea: and the third part of the sea became blood; And the third part of the creatures which were in the sea, and had life, died; and the third part of the ships were destroyed ... and the third part of the sun was smitten, and the third part of the moon, and the third part of the stars; so as the third part of them was darkened, and the day shone not for a third part of it, and the night likewise ... and I saw a star fall from heaven unto the earth ... And there came out of the smoke locusts upon the earth: and unto them was given power ... And the shapes of the locusts were like unto horses prepared unto battle: and on their heads were as it were crowns like gold, and their faces were as the faces of men. And they had hair as the hair of women, and their teeth were as the teeth of lions ... and the sound of their wings was as the sound of chariots of many horses running to battle. And they had tails like scorpions, and there were stings in their tails ...

Later, when I went to see you with a cup of coffee that seared my hand, I pictured the tubes in your mouth as a beak, a muscular beak so strong that it could cleave the earth to feed and live, and then you'd multiply until you filled all of Manhattan with a plague of your own DNA, repopulating the island after my fall in this apocalypse, which feels created specifically for me.

(I've been advised to tell you stories. I'll try to find some kinder ones. Although they also say it's the tone of voice that matters most, the feeling, the music of orality. I could recite the ingredients of a pre-cooked meal and it would work just as well.)

Day ten. You've been stable since your second cardiac arrest. Your grandmother left again and hasn't called. I've been told I need visitors, I need support. I have close friends in New York, but I don't want anyone to be startled at the sight of you. Because I do see fear in the faces of visitors to neighbouring incubators when they set eyes on their minuscule tenants for the very first time. Their expressions reveal a mixture of incredulity, admiration, pity, terror, bewilderment, and something else, as uncomfortable as it feels to say, that looks like rejection. But I don't blame them – I'm sure my own face flashed with all of those things the first time I saw you.

You're so thin, ChildOfMine: of course you'll startle anyone who's never seen a life simultaneously becoming and coming undone. Maybe 'raw' isn't the right word to describe your appearance. It's as if you lacked layers in your body, lining in your flesh, strata of muscle.

The ring on my finger would be too big for your arm. Maybe that's what I should warn anyone who wants to visit. *Hey, listen, before you go in to see her: the ring on my finger is too big for her arm.* I'd take off my ring and place it in the visitor's hand, and this would bring them at least a tiny bit closer to the reality of your improbable form. Yes, maybe this would prepare them better for what they're about to see. I can't be sure. In any case: here's the Lorca poem I promised to sing to you. I'll sing it to us:

> Mr Lizard is crying.
> Mrs Lizard is crying.
>
> Mr and Mrs Lizard
> in their little white aprons.
>
> They've gone and lost
> her wedding ring.
>
> Oh the little lead ring
> oh dear oh dear, the little lead ring! . . .
>
> Oh dear, how they cry,
> oh dear, oh dear, how they're crying![5]

Even before puberty hit, my mother was making me feel ashamed of my body. I can't remember when, but I was quite young when I started to hide my nakedness from her. She's never seen my breasts, never saw me naked in the transition from girlhood to adolescence or as a grown woman. But unluckily for me, when I started to pump my milk, my mother – who hardly ever came to visit – happened to be there. It wasn't until those postpartum days that she first saw my breasts. They didn't even feel like mine, their huge dark areolas all but unrecognisable to me, and my mother judged them with my life still in the balance. I felt repulsed. The same repulsion I'd experienced as a teenager when men my father's age would ogle my chest, drooling. Among all the serious obstacles I faced in those early hours, it amazed me that I could still feel ashamed of being naked in her presence. But I did. At certain moments, the weight of the gaze that openly derided my changing body was greater than my fear, as I massaged my breasts to stimulate the milk – which, adding insult to injury, wouldn't come in.

What little I can see of you is yellow. They tell me once again that this is normal. All things abnormal are normal here. Your liver is underdeveloped, so it struggles to process bilirubin. The blue light of your incubator is a special high-intensity light that helps break down bilirubin in the body and eliminate it through urine and faeces. This will help dissipate the yellowish tint in your skin and eyes. 'The eyes', the nurses say. And I ask myself: the eyes? What eyes?

MyChild, when will you find your form?

Before everything was suddenly reduced to sand dunes in the haziest regions of my history, I remember a childhood of ancient relatives: grandparents and even great-grandparents. They lavished me with so much love and attention that they're multitudinous in my memory, as if there were dozens of them, a hive where I was the royal jelly they all secreted, sticky and well-nourished with the richness of their affection. My great-grandmother Dolores could have filled the entire affective swarm all by herself. I find it perplexing and sad to have a daughter with no grandparents.

All I can offer you is the story of a grandfather who is crazy at best, and a grandmother who – well, I'm not sure about her yet. I'll need time to figure it out. People say that you understand your parents better when you become one yourself. In my case, the opposite is true. I understand them less. Much less. Will you understand me someday, when I tell you what I want right now: for you to cling to life? Even if your future is filled with pain, even if you turn out to be a consciousness lodged in an inert body, with a tongue that weighs heavy in your mouth? Maybe this makes me a worse mother than my own, but it's what I want:

Live.

Survive.

It's my first command as your mother.

One day, when I was five months pregnant and on holiday in Spain, I noticed in the bathroom that my knickers were soaked, as if I'd pissed myself. But I'd never experienced any leakage before, not even with the foetus bearing down on my bladder during pregnancy. Then it crossed my mind that it could be amniotic fluid. I panicked. By the time I realised, I was already running to the doctor's office. I say running because I really ran. I passed a bird that had fallen from its nest, but didn't stop, just kept running. I was late for my appointment, and figured I already had enough to worry about without rescuing animals. After a few seconds, though, it crossed my mind that the act of ignoring a defenceless life – refusing to help it – not only betrayed my beliefs about the relationship between humans and animals, but could also betray me, betray you. It was a kind of superstitious upwelling, an intuition of karmic justice. So I stopped, retraced, approached the bird and crouched down. Its eyes were closed, just like yours are now, but it was breathing. It was a sparrow chick, young, but old enough to have ventured out on its own with the appropriate precautions. I knew this because I'd collected many fallen birds as a child. Some survived, some didn't. I went into a nearby shop and asked for a cardboard box, and since it didn't have a lid, I decided to go into the appointment with the bird hidden in my hand. That's when I met my midwife, a woman who spoke to me with genuine kindness and interest, tended to me with her words. She asked me all the standard questions about my medical history in New York and I replied from across the table, my thoughts focused on the bird's heart beating inside the walls of my palm. It was hard to be in both places at once, but I could perceive the midwife's tenderness along with the vulnerability of the life I was concealing. Just as I was cradling a sick or wounded bird in my hand, it felt like the midwife was cradling me. And in my uterus, there you were, MyChild, who I couldn't protect. Because you weren't outside of me (in my hands) or in that office (in the midwife's hands), but inside me, inside a mother who felt profoundly fragile. At a certain point, I started to feel the little bird's heart rate slowing. I kept answering the midwife's queries, trying to mask my distraction, but soon the heartbeat had stopped altogether. As furtively as I could, I opened my hand and saw it was dead. I screamed. I can't remember what chaotic way I found to explain what had happened, but the midwife calmed me down, stood up and saw the bird for herself. Together, we placed it in a latex glove and then in a cardboard box, which we set down by the door. She helped me lie back onto the examining table and continued to soothe me, stroking my face and hands. And then I poured my heart out to her. I told her I didn't think I could carry MyChild much longer, didn't feel you were safe inside me, couldn't protect you properly; I was YourMother and if I felt this way, it had to be real – it wasn't just a feeling but a fact, a true intuition, and could she please tell me when I could get induced, I'd read about foetuses surviving in week twenty-five, you'd be safer in an incubator than inside me, I was broken, you were going to slip through the cracks of me at any moment, or else my panic attacks, my terrors, my nightmares would find a way to stop your heart, they'd kill you with an arrhythmia or a jolt of sorrow. The midwife, whose name was Sara, said you were already in the best possible place you could be. We listened to your heartbeat through a handheld doppler, and then she passed her hands over my belly, explaining how you were positioned, where your head was, your feet, your own little belly. You were moving around a lot, and Sara asked if you were always so active. You were, I said. 'Good. Movement is a sign of foetal wellbeing.'

It was the first time I felt that you might be able to make it inside me.

As I left the office, I picked up the cardboard box with the little bird wrapped in its latex cover. Once outside, I placed it in the first trash can I could find. I'd thought of burying it, but sometimes (this was certainly true of me just then) humanity is expressed through seemingly careless gestures. Giving the bird a more sophisticated send-off would have only shown that I was capable of a civilising act, and I wasn't. I felt more human precisely because all I could manage was to throw it away.

Calm seeped into my body like a chemical sedative. I could feel my panic slowly retreating, along with a sense of joy that expanded throughout the day.

MyChild, won't it be wonderful when I can read you things you'll understand? Like this passage about a woman named Yerma, who longs to have children and lives with the grief of not having them, and asks a pregnant woman how it feels to carry a baby inside her:

> 'What's it like?'
>
> . . .
>
> 'Don't ask me that. Haven't you ever held a live bird in your hand?'
>
> 'Yes.'
>
> 'It's like that. But in the blood.'[6]

When I learned about the existence of a device – a handheld doppler – used for listening to the foetus's heartbeat and even tracking its cardiac rhythm, I rushed to buy one and used it obsessively to make sure you were all right, your heart was running, your heart rate per minute was roughly similar to the previous day's. If I got nervous, I'd place the doppler on my belly and try to see if my nerves affected you. If I stopped feeling you move for more than two hours, I had to make sure you were still pulsing there. Sometimes I'd startle awake in the middle of the night and grab the doppler, which I always kept on my bedside table while I slept or in my handbag when I went out. In the aftermath of two miscarriages, I was terrified. And my mother – there was my mother too. If Sara the midwife had met my mother and known she was close by, maybe she wouldn't have been so confident that you'd make it to term.

As I've said, my mother stood on the threshold between my life and my death, and then she left me there. But there's more, much more. The most dramatic part is that she's the one who triggered my early labour. Before that, though, I want to explain something for context. It's something my mother also knew – which means she'd already seen me suffer so much that I believe I deserved some solace, even if only once in my life. After all, it took me four years to gestate you.

In the waiting room of the fertility clinic, where I spent most of my time in the weeks before my last embryo transfer, I saw women trying to conceive on their own, like I was, even if they had someone with them. They exuded a sadness that kept them lost in thought, not bothering to entertain themselves on their phones or flip through a magazine. It wasn't rude to refrain from greeting new patients when they came in. Silence was the norm, not exchanging smiles was the norm. Each of us would simply take a seat, maybe glance at the woman across the room, perhaps wondering idly what sort of fertility troubles had brought her there; how many years she'd spent pursuing a potentially impossible child, caring for herself as if she'd borne a foetus inside her for ages; what she'd given up; how many miles she was from home; if she'd managed to pay off her debts. Like me, those women had put their lives on hold ever since they decided they wanted to have a baby. From then on, we'd all been following the same routines: prenatal vitamins, no alcohol, no sugar, no lots of other things, tons of leafy green vegetables (spinach, kale, Swiss chard), avocados, moderate exercise, untold supplements meant to improve the quality of our eggs and endometrium. The market is infinite. We were also advised to cut gluten, according to recent studies that indicate it can compromise fertility. 'It's not yet proven,' the doctors say, but just in case, 'don't eat anything that contains gluten' (goodbye carefree restaurant dining, hello obsessive ingredient-analysis). All with the full knowledge that hormonal treatments may put us at risk of breast or ovarian cancer. What's more, the possibilities of developing some kind of cancer increase if you don't have a child in the end – which makes the child come to feel like both an allegorical and a literal salvation.

Some days before the egg retrieval, the nurses called to remind me not to use make-up, deodorant, or anything else that contains perfume. Such products could damage the eggs that would hopefully produce an embryo, initiating life in an incubator with a controlled environment that simulates conditions inside the uterus ... But it's not the uterus. It's not the uterus, and that's where my problem lay, my fear, my sleepless nights thinking about what the doctors had said: not even the very best laboratory can match the conditions of the reproductive system itself.

When retrieval day arrived, when the embryo was finally implanted in my uterus, I wanted to be sure that I'd done absolutely everything in my power to improve my odds. I didn't even use soap when I showered, and I was so nervous by the time I reached the clinic that I feared I reeked of sweat. I imagine this is quite a normal state of affairs; doctors must be used to the smell of fear, anxiety and expectation. The last time I'd had a miscarriage, as the doctor removed the final remnants of the foetus from my cervix, I caught the same distinctive smell: glands grieving for a baby that would never be, the fear of infinite infertility drifting through the operating room like a ghost that's fearful too, spraying its rancid stench about to spook the doctors and me. Alongside the doctor was one of those silvery cylindrical containers used to dispose of sanitary waste. I can still hear my own voice begging him as he worked between my legs, 'Please don't throw it away.' I repeated it several times, lots of times, not caring about the pain, or about the blood I heard spurting as if channelled through a pipe from my ravaged body. My mother was there that day, but she left then too (because, she claimed, she found the scene too hard to take). She said there was so much blood it was like they'd killed someone. Yes, Mama: they killed me.

When we got home, she said with scorn, 'I hope you don't try that again.' Not a single hug, not a single kiss, not a single word of comfort. At least she brought me dinner on the sofa that night before she locked herself in her room.

Of course I tried again. My doctor came into the room as I was already sitting on the table with a full bladder. Your bladder has to be full so that the cannula containing the embryo (containing you, this time) can enter more easily. The procedure feels so eternal that you invariably doubt your ability to hold your pee – to keep from wasting all those months of injections and effort over something as trivial as pissing yourself. But it'll be quick, they tell me. The doctor showed me a photo of your embryonic state, MyChild: a tiny round thing, five days old. Onscreen, I followed the cannula's path towards the uterus, where he planted you firmly – 'in a good spot,' were the doctor's exact words. He wished me luck as he left the office. From the doorway, having been informed about the medical mistreatment I'd experienced at a previous clinic, he said, 'You deserve this baby. You've worked hard for her.' And I started to cry. I cried because he was right. I did deserve you. I'd worked so hard to find you, as if you already existed. Of course, the idea of 'deserving' is banal and totally relative; there's no cause and effect that allows persistent people to get what they want. But I took the doctor's words in a more personal way. When he said I deserved my daughter, deserved you, it was like he could already see – before your birth, even before your conception – that I loved you, I'd take care of you. I was already a mother. And I wouldn't be like mine.

A nurse told me I was free to urinate after ten minutes had passed: the embryo wouldn't detach after that, as many women fear. Even so, I held it in for two more hours, just in case. Compared to everything I'd already been through, all the daily injections I'd given my bruise-mottled belly, a bursting bladder was nothing at all.

On my way back to the car, I remembered the esoteric-sounding advice I'd received a few days back from a friend who'd undergone the same process: 'To help the embryo implant properly, think of sticky things. For example, picture the embryo as a kind of jelly sticking to your endometrium. And eat pineapple, lots of pineapple.' I spent the whole flight back to New York in a panic, worried that every bout of turbulence would make it harder for you to hang on. Ten days later, I'd have a blood test to determine whether I was pregnant or not, or whether the hormone levels of your implantation were so weak that you'd become my third miscarriage.

I've never experienced anything as disturbingly obsessive as the determination to become a mother. If you feel it, nothing matters more. You'd sell your soul to the devil, and since that's impossible, lots of us sell whatever we have, even go into debt. If the child never comes, many are beset by years of depression. Sometimes it's less about the lack of a child than the knowledge that you'll never have the choice.

It hurts, being forced into nothing. You have to choose nothing or else it's torture. In this sense, it's like death.

I remember my last trip to the clinic. In the waiting room, eight women stared blankly out the window onto a scene from nowhere: green, perfect for not thinking any more than you have to. Another woman, the only other one who was standing, focused instead on an enormous aquarium. There was a sea urchin stuck to the glass wall. I looked too, studying a kind of blueish organ in the middle. It looked like an eye, but expanded and contracted like a pumping heart. When the woman left, I moved closer and gently touched the glass, standing there for a few moments, until a nurse called out a name and someone jumped and rushed to say, 'That's me,' as if someone else might try to usurp her role as future-possible-mother. Then she vanished through the door between the waiting room and the hall to the operating rooms. There she'd sleep for half an hour as the doctor extracted her eggs, and as four other doctors extracted the eggs from their respective patients. All asleep until it was time for the next women to go in, seized by fear and by the hope that, when they woke, they'd be told their eggs were viable: not too old or too immature or too few or unable to be fertilised. And then the pain, the bleeding, the nausea, the bruised ovaries, the mandatory bed rest, the risk of thrombosis, the very real sensation that, while they were sleeping, someone had been rummaging around in parts of their bodies that no one had ever touched.

My desire to have a child was more than a desire. It was more complex than that, perhaps too complex to explain at all. I'd always felt the need to give love, probably because it was my only way to believe I received it. Like feeding the hungry to satiate yourself. But it was about other things too. For one, the chance to see my own face when I was small. I've never really known what I looked like as a baby or very young child; my mother lost almost all of our family photos, and she was never good at describing my features. I don't think she even really remembered them. To me, having a child was a way to recover my own traits, forgotten by my mother, and the first tiny kicks with which I announced my life to the world, which my mother didn't feel – or which she found so insignificant that she's forgotten them as well.

At the first fertility clinic, I was wrongfully prescribed a medication used primarily to treat prostate cancer, which triggered early menopause. It lasted for six months. For obvious reasons, it was impossible for me to get pregnant by natural means. So much of my hair fell out that I wore a hat to cover up the bald patches. I felt so weak that I had to brush my teeth sitting down. My knees hurt so badly that I couldn't bear so much as a walk around the block. Around that time, I'd planned a trip to Tenerife with a friend. I didn't cancel it, but she had to carry me to the edge of the water if we wanted to go to the beach. The clinic denied that the injections they'd prescribed were the cause of my symptoms. I had to contact the lab, which confirmed that the medication was the culprit. By then I'd seen scores of doctors, undergone scores of tests, and received scores of diagnoses, from lupus to multiple sclerosis. Besides, due to the poor application of unnecessary hormones, I gained forty pounds. When I ran into acquaintances on the street and they saw the size of my belly, they congratulated me on the pregnancy I didn't have.

My mother is prone to friendships-at-first-sight. She's charismatic, makes a good impression. And she's chameleonic, skilled at adapting to other people's demands. But that's all it is: camouflage she uses to forge a bond she'll eventually need to break, for reasons I've never understood. My mother never lacks for a best friend, usually someone she met just a few days prior. Someone helpless in need of help. She tells me all about their trials and tribulations and how much she's supporting them. She truly invests her energy in other people. Sometimes she grants them refuge in her house. But when, after some time has passed, I ask her how so-and-so is doing, it turns out that they've already vanished from her life, always for a different reason, and are no longer relevant to her. One day, any ordinary day, as she's walking the dog or waiting in line at the post office, she'll meet her new best friend, and it starts all over again.

———

During the time when I was desperately trying to have a child, accepting all the physical and psychological consequences this entailed, I asked my mother not to tell anyone. I just didn't have the strength to talk outside the clinic about what was happening inside it, and inside me. I didn't want anyone to know anything except for my mother, and only because I stayed at her place for each treatment cycle. With all the changes in my physical appearance, I struggled to leave the house. It wasn't just all the weight I'd gained, but my palpable sadness. I felt ashamed of it. I didn't understand how I could let myself be annihilated by the desire to become a mother. If I hadn't experienced it myself, I'm not sure I would have understood it in other women. I had first-hand knowledge of cases in which a woman, told she'd never be able to conceive, had fallen into a deep depression, left her job for a few months, taken antidepressants, gone to therapy. And there I was, in the same place as each and every one of those women. At the same time, I was shocked that I'd come to disparage my own body and mental health in exchange for nothing, not even a child. So I wanted to go through the whole thing alone, in secret, play-acting for others that I was going about my normal life, and I asked my mother, begged her a thousand times, not to betray my confidence. I trusted her yet again. But one day, as we were watching TV, her latest best friend – one of those women my mother had just met – gave her a call. My mother thought I couldn't hear, but the speaker's voice on the other end of the line was so loud that I did: 'How's your daughter's treatment going?' My mother responded monosyllabically, faking it. And then the same voice asked, 'What about the menopause thing?' This lady wasn't a relative, not even a close friend. My mother had met her the week before. I grabbed the remote control and hurled it to the ground so hard that the batteries flew into the air.

When I was six months pregnant with you, only then did I start to believe you'd survive. And by the time everyone in my life had heard I was pregnant, I was so proud of my belly that I'd show it off whenever I could. I basically always wore low-riding trousers or skirts and short tops, so there was no mistaking the fact that there were two of us. I'd caress you through my belly all the time, at home and out and about, especially when I felt you moving. I liked communicating with you that way. One day my mother tugged down her trousers a bit, pulled up her shirt, and started to mimic me grotesquely, cackling, mocking the way I stroked my bump, mocking my pride in a belly that seemed, this time, at last, like it would make it to term.

I'll never forget this bitter, hateful ridicule. If she'd

known it would mark my memory of her forever, I don't think she would have done it. I recognised death in my mother's body that day. And if I could have imagined that she'd make herself hideous enough to imitate me, I wouldn't have looked. I'd have spared myself this glimpse of her in death, like a daughter who can't bear to look at her mother after a violent accident, desperate to protect the mental image of her living mother, immortal, intact, in full colour. In truth, though, I've always known: my mother's gruesomeness towards me is as infinite as death. As oblivion.

This morning, after several days of something like hope, you turned blue. The hall filled again with medical staff, and I thought this blue would never soften back into the raw pink of your birth, or the pink of the final protective skin you're supposed to keep developing. This blue was so blue that I didn't think it could possibly be removed without draping you in the cloak of death. I'd never associated such a colour with anything but the sea. Just a few days before we got here, when everything was physically going well for us, we floated in the Atlantic Ocean. You'd fallen asleep; I could tell the water had relaxed you. Then I dove down, holding my breath for a few seconds at the bottom, caressing the sand, watching a tiny hermit crab leave a trail. I turned a few pirouettes, blissful, weightless. Everything was so easy in the water. When I came out, I dried myself in the sun, and you slowly stirred from your oceanic nap. I stretched out not on a towel but directly on the sand, first on one side, then on the other, until it covered my whole body. That was the colour blue for me. And out of nowhere, this sense of possibility morphed into a gaping void, the sand swallowing us into the depths of the earth, ready to liquify us inside a nucleus of petroleum that no one will ever see.

'She's back,' said Dr Schol, and his words sent me tumbling out of the limbo where I stood transfixed by your blue. I missed the details of your resurrection.

Then they explained it again: the nervous systems of babies this premature haven't finished developing, so sometimes the brain doesn't receive the signal that their lungs need oxygen. This causes an apnoea that leads in turn to bradycardia, which makes their skin turn blue.

Before thirty-five weeks, they tell me, babies struggle to coordinate the simultaneous acts of sucking, swallowing and breathing. Sometimes you literally forget to breathe. What's just happened, they warn me, will probably happen again. I don't know how I'll be able to bear any more resurrections. If only I could know how many there were going to be. If only I knew they'd all be successful. If only my mother were here. If only I could forgive her. If only I could hit her.

I don't love my mother, Rilke confessed. Even though he spent years writing her letters of great tenderness, even though he must have loved her, he eventually said it: I don't love my mother. He wrote this poem after the last time they saw each other:

> Ah misery, my mother tears me down.
> I had fitted stone on stone to make me
> and stood already like a small house around
>   which the day moves spaciously,
> even all alone.
> Now Mother comes, comes and tears me down.
>
> Simply her coming and looking is enough.
> She doesn't see that someone builds.

She walks straight through my walls of stone.
Ah misery, my mother tears me down.

The birds circle me in lighter flight.
The strange dogs know: it's *him*.
Only my mother doesn't recognize–
my painstakingly fashioned face.[7]

I don't love my mother. Even though I must love her.

I've been told that a parent's love for a newborn pales in comparison to what that love becomes over the months and years. I can't imagine loving you more than I do right now. I don't even want to; it sounds impossible, pathological, unhealthy, a bomb of feeling that can't be good for anyone. On the other hand, if what they say is true, there's a silver lining: you're in an incubator at the very moment when my love for you hasn't stopped growing. I watch you develop every day – the changes are tiny, but I see them – and so the pulsing in my chest and stomach and uterus, where you're still supposed to be, is also getting stronger. Maybe nature is wise: you're this vulnerable because I don't yet love you as much as I could love you if you survive. That's why I can still bear it, as gruelling as it is. If I believe in this senselessness (and I want to believe), it means that if you live, I'll never have to see you again in the threshold between life and death, because I wouldn't survive it myself. The universe owes it to me that you grow up safe and healthy. This is the sort of nonsense I think. I have to cling to something, and right now I cling to a universe that doesn't exist. It doesn't exist, but I scream for it to let me keep holding on by a single finger, to keep me from plunging off the outer layer of the atmosphere.

Day fourteen. Yesterday I was discharged from the hospital and today I took my first full shower at home. I opened the door, set down my things on the kitchen table, and went into my room for some clothes to take back with me, preparing to spend as much time with you as possible. I slunk fearfully past your room, but then I retraced and stepped in. Everything is exactly as I left it: perfect, beautiful, ready to give you the warm welcome I imagined. But there's no baby. I open one of the dresser drawers. There is the diminutive onesie your grandmother gave me for your first day of life. I pick it up. It's soft. The set is completed by a pair of tiny mittens, to keep you from scratching your face, and a pink hat. It's pink because I wanted everything to be standard, orderly, normal, cliché. Fear forces us into the safest place. I pack the outfit and imagine spreading it out on top of the incubator, so you'll see it when you open your eyes, and so I can picture you wearing these clothes as you struggle with all your might to fill them. I don't want to look much longer. I strip down, dispose of my still-bloody nappy and step into the shower. It's the first time I've been apart from you since they started letting me spend night and day by the incubator, but I'm grateful for the water streaming over my body. I watch it slip down the drain, rust-coloured, littered with clots and unidentifiable bits of myself. The remnants of birthing a baby who should still be inside me. I'm reminded of a puzzle. Maybe some of these fallen scraps belong to you, like the blue pieces that belong to the sky; maybe they're essential to the proper functioning of your kidneys or your hearing. MyChild, an unfinished puzzle. I wash my hair for the first time, apply a face mask, sit down by the drain as it swallows everything that comes out of me and break into desperate sobs – also for the first time. Maybe part of your liver, flecks of your eyelashes are already coursing down into the pipes, into the sewers of Manhattan. Ever since I first witnessed one-pound babies with my own eyes, I've believed that anything is possible.

When you arrived, I dissolved. I know I got up because I'm not lying down. I know I brushed my hair because I've got two clips pulling back my hair. I know I've eaten because I see scraps of food in the rubbish bin on the rare occasions when I go home. But I don't know what else happens when I'm apart from you. I live in you. I'm the bacteria growing in a dying body. The buzzard, ignorant to own flight, engrossed in the carrion below. I know what I'm writing is awful. If you don't make it, I think I'll turn bad. I'll become a bad person.

After a few sporadic visits to the hospital, my mother travelled back to Spain without telling me. Since then, she appears to have begun an unprecedented new chapter as a volunteer. This involves driving a Red Cross truck through the streets of Málaga, distributing food to unhoused people. It must please her to say that she's volunteering. I'm sure she especially likes the bit about the truck, which makes it more evident;

the Red Cross truck is far more visible than a T-shirt. Besides, a T-shirt doesn't necessarily make you a volunteer, since it could be borrowed or handed down. Driving the truck means you get to shout it from the rooftops.

My mother has never been consistent about anything, but there are two things she's always aspired to: being liked and coming off as a good person. It's interesting to me that she's chosen a lie to achieve this goal, a false identity. Wouldn't it make more sense to do good because you really need to, or want to, or because helping others comes naturally to you? Why work so hard to act as if you care about other people if you actually don't? What's the appeal? The world is full of selfish people who don't bother hiding their selfishness. Why not belong to that world, which so readily belongs to her? Why struggle to construct an honourable image of yourself when you could simply act with honour?

Maybe my mother proclaims her false goodness while driving a truck around Málaga because here, in this hospital, only a handful of doctors and nurses are around to take in the show. It's too small an audience. Besides, my mother likes going out. Being out. And we're locked up.

It was my grandmother who taught me to cook. My mother was an expert at making a single recipe for an ancient sauce once prepared by the Romans, among other peoples:

If you don't have a tub, use a clay jug with a twenty-to-thirty-litre capacity.

Extract the guts and other discardable parts of

certain blue fish, primarily tuna, morays, sardines, or mackerel.

From the larger fish, remove the liver, intestines, roe, milt (sperm-containing fluid), throats and blood.

Leave the smaller fish intact.

Aromatic herbs of your liking: spearmint, fennel, dill, oregano, coriander, celery, etc.

Large quantities of salt.

Fill the jug as follows:

First, to form a base at the bottom of the clay vessel, make a layer of aromatic herbs.

Next come the smallest fish (remember: intact).

The second layer consists of larger fish parts, as mentioned above.

Cover with a thick layer of salt, which will serve as an antiseptic and prevent bacterial rotting.

Repeat the order of ingredients until the jug is completely full.

Cover the jug and let it ferment in the sun for a week.

For twenty days, stir the mixture until it reduces (although the process may be sustained for several months).

The final result is the much-prized *garum*, a sauce the Romans deemed more precious than the finest perfume.

My mother recounted this recipe and its history as if she'd learned it by heart. She'd just modify the quantity of condiments as the circumstances required. While pregnant with me, she often said, she sometimes cried so much that her food tasted salty. I think my mother actually mastered ancient salting techniques to preserve her own pain. She places her guts in a jug, conserves their bitterness, lets them ferment, periodically uncorks the vessel for me to sniff.

But I don't know if this pain even exists for her, or if she ferments it for me alone. In any case, my mother's taste is a bitter one.

My mother is a sun that doesn't warm. Better put, my mother is a sun that saves her heat for others. She works hard to shine for everyone else. Whenever I've needed her, seeking her out like a lizard longing to rest on a bright patch of ground in springtime, her light and warmth have shifted away. I'm capable of moving the sun. Why didn't this cross my mind when I was small? However illusory, the thought that I possessed such a superpower might have been a comfort. But none of my fantasies could fool me; my mother has always been a sun that fled as soon as I approached. I think of the beach again. My cousin's beach. The beach that tugs at me – that's what it seems to do, given how often I'm reminded of it – to teach me something. In the castle of my mind, I sift its sand together with the sand of the beach where, many years ago, although it was really just a few days back, I went into early labour.

The nurses take good care of you. It's like you're tucked into a nest of sundry cables they entwine like busy birds concerned about my little chick. They work deftly, as if prompted less by technique, studies, and years of medical experience than by instinct; some age-old wisdom that dates back to cavewomen keeping the fire alive. The nurses prepare the nest with twigs that channel oxygen and other unspecified things. At the same time, they keep your nest as warm as the first mother's womb. You contribute too: you let yourself be cared for. Which is no small feat; after all, you're still here. According to neuroscience, thoughts and senses are determined by mere electrochemical reactions between neurons. But when I look at you, as diminutive a surface area as your body covers, you seem to be made of sheer soul. It's not a very scientific image, and yet, for now, your will to live appears to weigh more than your flesh and bones.

The baby in the third incubator has just arrived. I can't figure out what, but something seems to be wrong with her respirator. Her lungs are collapsing. I don't want to look, I shouldn't look, but I do. Only her chest moves. Struggling, she has only enough energy to try and take air into her lungs. She's lying face up, and if it weren't for her motionless arms and legs, she'd look like a strange fish out of water, grappling for oxygen, her gills flaring and pressing shut in a state of agony. Her sweat-filmed body is turning grey. Five or so doctors and nurses, the very best, renowned in their fields, decide to rush her out of the hall. I don't know where they take her, but I never see her again. I don't ask. Questions are excessive; there's much more information in here than what we want to know. But it does cross my mind that if you should take a sudden turn for the worse, you'll need some of the medical staff who just ran out with the other baby. And I hope (forgive me) that everything will be over for her quickly, if end it must, so that they'll be back as soon as possible.

The orderlies wash the glass walls of your incubator with great care. With equilibrium, you might say, as if strapped into a harness to keep them safe while washing the windows of a skyscraper. You could even say that they clean the incubator as if it were your skin. They caress the dust away.

This care, this incredible effort to spare you even the slightest discomfort, makes me think of Jainist doctrine, which has sought for centuries to keep from harming any living things, insects included. Some ascetics sweep the ground as they walk, using brushes with very soft bristles to move aside ants and beetles without hurting them. They also wear face masks so as not to harm flying insects. My tiny baby, they protect you as if you were as vulnerable as the wings of a butterfly in Jainist India.

It's five a.m. Everything around me is quiet and calm. But I can't sleep. I dreamed something, and maybe this dream I can't recall has made me stir, reminding me of a book that made a strong impression on me some years back. It was by a young Swiss man who was dying as he wrote it. I Google the book and find the beginning, which the thirty-two-year-old author wrote when he was informed of his illness: 'I'm young and rich and well-educated . . . I come from one of the very best families on the east shore of Lake Zurich . . . My upbringing has been middle-class, and I have been a model of good behaviour all my life . . . And of course I have cancer.'[8]

The author interprets his illness as a logical response to the spiritual troubles of the West. He sees it as a symptom with no relation to his genetic information, a practically environmental cause: cancer as a consequence of prolonged exposure to radioactive morals and a lifestyle that can only culminate in death.

A year after the publication of Fritz Zorn's only book, in the middle of a summer night on the island of Cavallo, an Italian prince named Vittorio Emanuele of Savoy shot and killed, apparently by accident, a nineteen-year-old boy sleeping on the deck of an adjacent yacht. The young man's father, the physician Ryke Geerd Hamer, got cancer soon after his death, and he too identified his illness as an affliction of the soul. As a result, the doctor developed a medical theory in which a physical cure is only possible through the resolution of spiritual conflict. Following this theory, many people abandoned their treatments, many died, and Hamer's medical licence was revoked.

I wish I had some eccentric, collective explanation for the state I see you in. In any case, I understand that physical health and overall wellbeing are linked. I myself blame my mother for your suffering. My mother is your illness, my mother is the ill of all the West.

And yet I sometimes wonder what would happen if one day, in weeks, months, or years, my mother wanted to be a good grandmother, and I gave her a chance, and she proved that she really could be good and kind to you, even if she wasn't for me. Shouldn't I then forget about everything I'm writing here and give you a grandmother? But where does my mother end and your grandmother begin?

My gaze is like a fly on the monitor that shows me your vital signs. I stare at that screen whenever I'm not blankly reading the same line ten times in a book

I never finish, or when I'm not Googling some detail I haven't fully understood, because when the neonatologist explained it to me I was still trying to make sense of the previous complication, which I didn't fully understand either, because I'd been trying to get my head around the second-to-last explanation, and so on. I know what the parameters are supposed to be:

Heart rate: 100/200 bpm.

Temperature: 36.5 °C/37.5 °C.

Oxygen saturation: 85/100%.

You preemies are in especially urgent need of calm, and you're so sensitive to external stimuli that any sudden noise in the hall, however inevitable, causes your oxygen saturation to plunge. An alarm sounds. But then the number instantly rises and stabilises within normal parameters if I whisper or croon to you. It seems easy to make you happy when I see these figures, but it also seems too easy for the slightest thing to send you spiralling into crisis, halt your breathing with any ordinary noise.

Like a fly. My gaze, hovering on the screen, is like a fly, because I too have alighted in the lines of the book I've been reading for the past two days. Two days between these lines and the screen with your constant vitals:

> A fly was bothering me. I'd shoo it away, but it kept coming back, so I shooed it again.
>
> 'No, huh? All right, then, I'll wait for –'
>
> It drifted away a bit and landed on a dead dog.
>
> 'For what?' I asked.
>
> It didn't reply. And I didn't insist, fearing that I already knew the answer.[9]

IV

27 WEEKS

29 OUNCES

(The Beach)

People find it strange that I make the bed and clean the bathroom whenever I stay in a hotel. Why bother, if that's what housekeepers are for? I can't say it's out of solidarity, it's not to reduce their workload, although I'm glad if it does. The real reason is that whenever I step into a place where I'm going to sleep for more than a night, I need to make it mine, mine as if it were my own home, be it a hotel room, my office or a camping tent. Now, in this hospital hall filled with premature infants, I look around and consider what I'd rearrange.

When I open the door to a hotel room, a sense sharpens in me: the sense of space, of possible wellbeing, of an emotional architecture. I see plants that aren't there, flowering beside a cat as it suns on the sill. I see my favourite duvet, my eternal teapot on top of my desk. I don't see the suitcases I've dragged around for hours of travel. The wardrobes are already orderly. As soon as I open the bathroom door, the toothbrush, deodorant and compresses are perfectly in place. I don't see some impersonal hotel room where a stranger will stay once I've gone; I see a home for me, forever. Obviously, these sensations are part of me, maybe even a kind of disorder, one I've never cared to think too hard about, since it hasn't caused me any harm. Right now, though, it does feel harmful, because as I look around this room, which isn't in a hotel but in a hospital, I inhabit it as if I'll be here forever, as much as I wish I could escape. That's how powerfully I need to root myself, to belong.

I think I know when I started needing to make any temporary space my own. It was when, at fourteen, I learned I'd soon be without a place to live, and I started spending hours compulsively copying out my full address on little scraps of paper. There were dozens of them everywhere, as if the repetition could redeem me as it did at school, ordered to write down some trivial offence again and again as punishment. My mother, in the name of depression, had fled to my grandparents' house in a distant city. She was almost cheerful when she returned. That year, I realised I'd become my own sole caretaker, with all the struggles and loneliness that this implied.

A friend told me recently that he'd set some lentils to soak, drained the water and seen a tiny green shoot peering up from the grate. A carelessly discarded lentil had taken root in the gloomy pipes of a New York sink. That's what it's like for me: not a drive to occupy, but a need to settle.

The first time my mother left, I wasn't orphaned, but abandoned. Have you ever seen pictures of a shark tossed back into the sea alive after its fins have been cut? It's a good symbol for loneliness. Restored to its habitat, the animal tries to correct its downward plunge, but it can't: where it had fins mere seconds before, now it has only a set of purpled incisions, and it keeps falling down and down like a slow torpedo until it hits the ocean floor. There it stays, with its eyes rounder, more open than before, opening and shutting its mouth as blood seeps from its gills like intermittent spurts of diluted ink, spelling out a message no one will answer. And there it will remain for a good long while, subsumed in loneliness, paralysis, hunger.

———

Deep down, loneliness and hunger are similar; just as hunger isn't merely the absence of food on a day of fasting, loneliness isn't the occasional lack of company. Both entail a biochemical imbalance, a persistent misalignment of the self, in such a way that when food finally enters our stomachs or a hug envelops our bodies, we already carry the virus of absence inside us. It's like the shingles virus, which goes dormant but doesn't die. And one day, when you've enjoyed a good meal with lifelong friends, a diminutive blister emerges on your side, then many more blisters spread like a snake, and you lower your head, crestfallen, and if someone asks why you look so sad at such a joyful gathering, the honest answer would be: I'm alone. It's hard to explain how loneliness crept into you long ago, and no antiviral drug can cure you forever. Shingles reawakens with the sun, synonymous with energy and life. Loneliness can stir in the same conditions, even when you're feeling at your best. That's why it doesn't depend on whether you're alone or not, but on how emotionally stunted you were in the past.

———

Day twenty-four. On the days when you seem stable, the doctors say it'll do me good to get out. I've heard this a million times, and maybe it's true. I know I know I know, I need to take care of myself so I can take care of you. But today I go out and the city doesn't feel the same. I don't know what to do, so I go to our neighbourhood launderette, close enough to the hospital for me to rush back if something happens. Maybe I've also chosen the launderette because it can be good to do something mechanical, one of those little things that people claim will help you weather catastrophe by focusing on ordinary, meditative gestures: the mother who makes hundreds of origami cranes as the rescue squads search for her child among the ruins of the nuclear plant. And here I am, sitting before a row of industrial washing machines in three different sizes, with another row of dryers behind me. I count them. Forty washing machines. Thirty dryers. All lining a long, narrow space like an alleyway of stunned eyes.

I have no idea how long I've sat here watching clothes spin, so swiftly that they look like a single smear of colour inside the machines. Finally I come back to earth and shift into a less stagnant form of meditation. I take the dirty clothes I've been accumulating all week in my locker at the hospital. I choose a medium-sized machine. As I open the door, I realise I don't have any change on me, just a ten-dollar bill, which I insert into the quarter dispenser. The machine rejects it. I did it wrong, Alexander Hamilton is supposed to face up – an ugly fellow, he'd be better off face down, but whatever, I try it again. The machine spits it out once more. The bill must be wrinkled. I smooth out the corners. I insert it again, and this time the coins rain down, rattling like hail against the frame of a cheap car.

I collect the coins one by one, not like I usually do, scooping them up with both hands. One by one now, slowly. When I turn around, I see that the owner, a woman from El Salvador who rarely says much but is always kind and attentive to what's going on in the launderette, has noticed. She's noticed that I'm no longer pregnant and that it's too soon for me to have given birth. She looks at me with more compassion than curiosity, asking nothing. This is New York. 'Mind your own business' is the law of the land.

I return to the washing machines and select number ten. Little by little, I load my clothes. I used to feel self-conscious about other customers seeing my underwear; I'd glance furtively around, always dropping some garment or other as I emptied the bag. Now I don't even bother checking to see if anyone's nearby when I pull out my bloodstained postpartum underwear. One, two, three: in they all go. I'm still bleeding, still need them. Next comes a couple of bras, now too big for me; a set of blue pyjamas stamped with yellow tigers I fell in love with at first sight and bought for myself, imagining our first days together at home; and not much else – a T-shirt, some other outdoor clothes. A few garments were left at the bottom of the bag, and I stood motionless for several moments, wondering whether or not to wash them. A few of your own clothes that the nurses have changed and I've kept so I can smell them, touch them. Tiny socks, tiny hats. Finally I decide to add all of your things to mine in the machine. It's a kind of superstition, a way to say: I'm going to wash them because you'll be out of the hospital soon and I won't need any relics of yours.

Once I'm done filling the machine, I shut the door, round as an eye staring into the hurricane and insert the coins – mechanical gestures that soothe me once more. I take my time, ignoring the woman behind me, whose impatience and obliviousness prompt her to murmur some insult I can't quite make out. I glance to one side and catch an accidental look at myself in a mirror. My God. I hadn't expected the deep mauve hollows under my eyes, my air of stray mammal, too thin to have just given birth, too pale to be food. No, I don't look like someone whose milk could possibly nourish another human being.

Just as I was taking in my wrecked, dismantled appearance, Katy called and told me to come back right away. Her tone suggested that the news wasn't bad, although I couldn't imagine how good it could be. Here, the only possible positive thing is that nothing negative happens, in which case she wouldn't call with such urgency. But of course, your eyes, why didn't I think of that? You'd opened your eyes. I practically sprinted into the ward without a word to anyone, and I saw you. They were so small that I couldn't see the white part: your eyes, two diminutive spheres, dark and intense and expressive. I don't know what they said, MyChild, but they spoke. Maybe they were saying: Now I can't die anymore, or now I feel pain. I don't know, I don't know, but in that moment I was utterly certain that the worst was over. The nurses gathered, gazing down at you brightly, and you shifted your arms in the air as if you'd noticed the change. But I don't know, I don't know anything, who could possibly know, I just wanted to put it in writing: you opened your eyes, and lots of people came to celebrate. Today was your first party. Your first birthday party, perhaps.

Your eyes emerged. Two of them. Wide open. Exactly where they're supposed to be. They feel to me like the eyes of the world.

Your skin still looks as delicate as the outside of a silvery depth-dwelling insect, the kind that disintegrates at the slightest touch. That's why the nurses remove all the devices from your face once a day, to make sure your skin is still properly in place. But you're alive, you're here. And you have eyes. Open eyes. That's what I tell myself every morning before I open my own eyes on this sofa, mere centimetres away.

You dislike being washed. The realisation that something bothers you is another tremendous step. Maybe you've tried before, but I hadn't grasped it until today: even though you're still unable to make any specific gestures or whimper or issue any other interpretable sound, you communicate by secreting a very specific, highly intense odour that disperses through the room like the spores of a fungus. When you know you're about to be washed, you smell. You smell every time you dislike something. Today a nurse brushed a tiny bandage across your lips and your whole body contracted. Don't scarring wounds also contract? I'm happy. I let myself feel happy.

In recent days, I've often wondered how long I could keep considering you a baby. It's been over three weeks, but sometimes it still seems like you're vacillating between death and thingness, not life and death. Which is why, if I see that your nappy is wet, that it contains something like urine or faeces, I'll tell myself: She's human, and she's my daughter. Today it happened again. All good news. I celebrate each bowel movement as an act of life.

During my great-grandmother Dolores's last days of life, I'd clean her mouth after every meal. I'd wrap a finger in gauze and slip it along her tongue and gums, the furrows where her teeth had been, stimulating her saliva; I'd remove my finger every two or three seconds for her to breathe, then go on. I felt her ulcerations, learned the size of each one. When she breathed continuously through her mouth, a membrane would form that seemed to block her throat. It was like the flimsy skin inside an eggshell. I'd tug and it would come out whole, dissolve on contact with my fingernails. That's what your skin reminds me of. There are lots of similarities between the prenatal void and the void after life.

Today I felt an optimistic urge to show you off, send my mother a message: Fuck you, she's going to live in spite of you, and she's beautiful. I did this by sending her a photo of you with your new eyes open. I texted it to my Aunt Carmen for her to forward to my mother. But I did something I'm ashamed of: I altered the photo. I fattened your arms and legs a little. In part because my mother has always judged my appearance, and I'm stupid enough to fall into her trap and modify the photo of my microbaby so she won't judge you too. Now I regret it; it stands as evidence that I cared more about my mother's perception – I wanted her to see a more fully finished baby – than about defending you exactly as you are. I still care about my mother, and I hate that she's still powerful enough to affect my behaviour. But I forgive myself. Today is a day for celebration.

Whenever Dr Truong stops in, I worry he's coming more to see how one of us mothers is doing than to check on our children. It terrifies me when the doctors or nurses start to offer palliative care for us. You can tell by how they move, the look in their eyes, the way they say goodbye to a baby, thinking we don't register the change. They do this when it's too soon to announce a proximate death: nothing is certain, and miracles happen often enough that they won't preempt the end. Resurrections happen. Resurrections happen every day. I've seen them. In you, in other babies. Every single day.

At the end of a day filled with good news, they've decided to remove your high-frequency ventilator. The nurse croons to you tenderly as she works. It's an incredible step towards respiratory freedom. I watch her adjust the settings, gradually reducing the pressure and rate of your breathing cycles. The rumble of the machine grows fainter and bids us farewell with a whisper of air.

Now they fit you with something called a CPAP machine. It's much smaller than the previous one, and all they need to do is adjust it to your nostrils and secure it with a bit of surgical tape. There's no more noise. You don't vibrate anymore. They won't have to sedate you so much. I watch you breathe practically unassisted. Little by little, the nurse tells me, your lungs will gain strength and flexibility. Every breath trains your lungs. You're a prenatal athlete.

Now you're closer to the air of the world.

During my pregnancy, I never felt the urge to read anything about how to help my body give birth. Even so, I stumbled across information that stuck with me. One detail surprised me with its visual force: we're all born premature.

This is true even if our mothers carry their pregnancies to term. I'll explain: contrary to everything we're told (your body knows what to do, women have been doing this for thousands of years without any need for hospitals, etc.), human childbirth is among the most difficult, even lethal forms of birth in nature.

In order to see from a certain height and use their hands, hominids had to start walking upright. In this way, they could survey the horizon, hunt more effectively and gather fruit. But there was a price to pay. The path towards upright posture brought about aches and pains and back trouble. Women suffered the brunt of these changes. To walk on two legs, the hominid skeleton had to reconfigure itself, which narrowed the pelvis. At the same time, the human brain grew, so foetuses' heads got larger and larger. This led to an obstetric dilemma. Two opposing forces pulled on the woman's pelvis: on the one hand, its narrowing, which let her walk vertically; on the other, the need for a broader birth canal, so she could birth babies with bigger heads. While the birth canal is practically straight in primates, the human birth canal became warped, curved, complicating the process for both woman and baby. Death in childbirth became more frequent. Natural selection, in all its impartial wisdom, started inducing untimely births – an evolutionary response to ensure a greater survival rate for mothers as well as their children. That is, babies had to be born before their heads grew too large. In other words: prematurely. All it takes is a glance at a newborn to see how helpless they are in comparison to other mammals.

'We're all born premature': this grants you an even greater level of precocity, one so dangerous that nobody would have survived it just decades ago. Your existence is only possible today thanks to the incubator, which serves to replace my uterus. You've emerged from my birth canal and returned to a uterus that isn't mine. And if you'd been born in an under-developed country, neither of us would be alive right now. As with just about everything, prenatal survival is a question of economic geography.

My gynaecologist advised me to put my birth plan in writing. I'd always thought about childbirth without fear. In fact, I saw it as the end of a different fear – the fear of loss, following several miscarriages – and it hadn't crossed my mind to plan anything out. For some reason, labour was the only part I thought would turn out just fine if I managed to keep you inside me for the full nine months. That's why I never attended any birth preparation courses or read any books. In response to my doctor's recommendation, though, I sought out some more information and sent her a list of preferences:

Vaginal birth.

Unmedicated birth.

No epidural.

Avoid episiotomy unless a matter of life and death.

Avoid C-section unless absolutely medically necessary.

If a C-section is required, I want to remain conscious.

I want to have my mother with me the whole time.

Freedom of movement during labour (walking, standing, sitting, crouching, etc).

Avoid the use of forceps and suction unless absolutely necessary.

Delay clamping and cutting of the umbilical cord until it's no longer pulsating.

I'd like to have skin-to-skin contact with my baby as soon as possible after birth.

I'd like to breastfeed my baby as soon as possible.

If the doctors need to take my baby away from me for any reason, I want my mother to accompany my baby and remain present during all procedures.

Water is important to me; if possible, I'd like to spend most of the contractions in the shower.

I'd like dim lighting during labour.

I want to use a mirror to watch my daughter being born.

Thank you,
M.

Nearly fifty per cent of all premature births are idiopathic. The woman goes into labour unexpectedly and the doctors don't know exactly why.

But I'm convinced you came early due to a shock, a fright my mother gave me. It went straight to my womb. What I learn from Dr Truong only bolsters this theory. During the first few days, I didn't ask, too scared to confirm that my mother may have been the cause of our suffering. But when I finally did, he explained: cortisol, the so-called stress hormone, can diminish progesterone in utero. The reduction of progesterone due to the increase of cortisol – stress – triggers contractions. That's why women with high stress levels often go into labour far before term: days, weeks, or, in my case, months.

What's more, when adrenaline skyrockets, the body musters all of its resources to survive, sacrificing a pregnancy it may not be able to handle in favour of saving the mother's life.

But there's something else: cumulative stress, the stress a person may experience since childhood and adolescence and sustain during their adult life, also takes a toll. Cumulative stress reduces life expectancy, and thus affects gestation too. A physically healthy forty-year-old woman who hasn't faced any major struggles in her life has greater chances of carrying a healthy pregnancy to term than a much younger woman who's been subjected to significant stress or trauma since girlhood.

On the day we returned from the beach, my mother, who had always been my source of cumulative stress, also became a source of specific stress when she pushed me into a situation of panic, of danger, of having to save my life and my pregnancy. This is what happened. We'd gone to Fire Island, a beautiful nature preserve where deer roam free and natural dunes separate the reed beds from the white-sand beaches. It was a lovely day of sunbathing and fresh air. I stretched out on the hot sand to feel the salt dry on my skin, tautening it with a feeling of both pleasure and discomfort.

I was tired as we got ready to head home, and we decided my mother would drive. Around the halfway point, we started arguing, though I can't even remember why, it was nothing serious, but my mother went into full-blown hysteria mode right there on the highway, one of the most dangerous in New York. I asked her to drive carefully. Next thing I knew, she grabbed a water bottle that was lying around in the car, uncapped it, stuck it into her mouth and acted as if she were choking. She coughed, still driving, refusing to pull over. I couldn't throw myself out of the moving vehicle, but I thought about it. Even if she was putting on a show, which I suspected, she devoted herself so single-mindedly to making the choking fit seem real that she stopped paying attention to the road. She drove fast, lurching wildly as other cars honked. I tried to stay calm. I patted her hard on the back, she spat out the cap, I asked if she was feeling better, I gave her the attention she craved, she relaxed a bit. I told her to please stop at the next petrol station, I needed to use the bathroom.

It was at the petrol station that my waters broke. Three months and three weeks early.

My mother was the very definition of stress: sudden contractions, the rupture of the amniotic sac, the severance of the cord that connected us.

I'd always demanded her love. Maybe I was still demanding it when your head peeked out of my vagina without me knowing if you were dead or alive. But when she left, on top of everything else she'd done, my mother became my enemy. It's not that I don't love her. It's that I find it impossible to love her. And when your flesh and blood does you so much harm, there's no middle ground: it's love or hate. Although of course it's always really love, love in the form of hate, which is the worst form of both.

If I didn't know that my mother was cruel, I'd think she was stupid. I used to believe that she wasn't very intelligent, which is why I forgave the blows she tried to pass off as accidents and oversights, as if she'd tripped on a rock – except I was both the rock and the fall. But ever since she stuck a water bottle cap into her mouth and pretended to choke while driving, and ever since – as if that weren't enough – she went away, leaving us at risk of death, I believe my mother is only cruel. Or at least more cruel than stupid.

My cousin, lost on the beach when I was six and she was three. My cousin, buried in a cemetery in Seville. A chubby, cheerful little girl with curly blonde hair, her photo always on display in the cosiest spot of every relative's home. But no one could ever speak of her. I learned this early, the first time I asked. She was my cousin. So where was she? Silence. After that day on the beach, no one ever told me anything.

My aunt. My Aunt Carmen calls. My mother received the photo. I have to forgive her. Which is why my aunt has apparently decided to tell me the family secret: it's a deal for forgiving my mother.

She and my uncle had moved to Germany in search of work and left my cousin Lucía, three years and three months old, in my parents' care, so that she could enjoy a few summery weeks under the Andalusian sun. One day, the whole family went to the beach. It was one of those Huelva beaches with a pine forest rising up past the strip of sand; the air smelled of resin mixed with the salt of the sea. My little cousin had never seen the ocean before and got to delight in it for the first time. Besides my parents, my grandparents, older cousins, two of my uncles and another aunt were there. Everyone kept an eye on her. She was the baby of the family, and they wanted to make sure she had a sweet, happy time in Spain, universally coddled before she went back to Germany, where there were no relatives except for her parents. My mother loved taking her into the water, and since she'd always been the best swimmer in the family, everybody trusted her. My cousin loved it, asked to be taken back again and again. I'm setting this down as my aunt told it to me; I have no memories of my cousin that day. I do recall a day at the beach with all the others, but I don't remember her. I also remember my mother in the water with me, playing, teaching me to plunge under whenever a big wave was about to hit. In any case, my aunt tells me, after one of these dips in the sea, my mother brought my cousin back to their towels for a snack. With all these brand-new stimuli coursing through her, the luxurious exhaustion that follows a swim and a full belly, my little cousin fell asleep wrapped snug in my mother's arms. It was only when my mother woke up that she realised she'd fallen asleep herself. And when she didn't see my cousin there, she wanted to think that the child was with some other member of the family. But she must have feared something right away, because she screamed. Everyone came running, both my relatives and beach-going strangers. No one knew where my cousin was.

Curiously, when I read my birth plan now, I realise that many of my wishes came true: I did have a vaginal birth, no medication, no epidural, no episiotomy, no forceps. Other preferences proved impossible: where I'd dreamed of dim lighting and a calm environment, I had glaringly bright lights trained on me from all directions. Doctors and nurses rushed in and out. Where I'd longed for a hushed, shadowed labour, you came into the world amid the greatest stress I'd ever experienced. Skin-to-skin contact wasn't meant to be, either: you were whisked away at once, and as they wheeled me down the hall on a stretcher and I overheard 'We're going to try to save them both,' I feared that my skin and your skin would never meet again. I asked about you as they tended to me, but no one would tell me anything, just that I needed to keep calm.

I forgot something crucial in my birth plan. Something worse than an episiotomy, where they cut into the tissue between your vagina and your anus; worse than forceps; worse than the most obvious cases of obstetric violence. What I should have included was a restraining order against my mother.

Now that my daughter has started to need more food, my milk is essential. I do have some, but it never amounts to more than a couple of spoonfuls, so I need to increase stimulation. I've been assigned a lactation consultant who doubles as one of our primary nurses. I'd seen several such consultants working with other mothers, but they always struck me as members of a sect, both reserved and nearly violent in their way of demanding another woman's milk. Mine is very different, though. Her name is Adrianne and part of her face is covered in indecipherable tattoos. Gentle to the point of affectionate from the very beginning, she shows interest in my mental state. She takes a seat, offers me a glass of water, makes light conversation. A great relief. Then she asks me to show her my breasts. I open my robe and carefully start to massage them. Some of my ducts appear to be slightly blocked. Adrianne applies hot compresses that smell like a forest, like oil extracted from some aromatic herb. She asks me to lean back in the armchair and try to relax, and she presses in a circular motion with her index and ring fingers. It doesn't hurt. I genuinely feel as if my breasts were resting, releasing tension at last. Half an hour passes this way, and it's the first time since I got here that I've been able to connect with my body, even for a few moments.

'We're going to get that milk of yours. Even more than you need,' Adrianne says. I like her optimism. Then she tucks a lock of hair behind my ear and asks what I'd like to eat. Eat? It's true, I've barely eaten in days. A cheeseburger and a big glass of milk, I tell her. 'Great choice,' she says. 'You need the calories.'

Before she leaves, Adrianne explains the next steps. She'll visit my room every two hours and take me to the lactation area, where, she repeats, 'We're going to get lots of milk out.'

I eat my hamburger with a hunger I haven't felt since I arrived. Then I take the glass of milk, pour it meticulously into the plastic container that collects the scant droplets the pump has wrested out of me and send the photo – as if it were my harvest – to my mother. 'My milk came in,' I text her.

It's another lie that fills me with shame. How obviously I still crave my mother's approval. She spent her brief visit mocking my efforts to recover the milk she insisted would never come in. But after hearing my aunt's story, I feel something different for her now, something like understanding. Something like an apology, even, however small, however faint. The onset of another feeling I can't yet name.

My aunt's story continues. Once it was clear that my cousin had gone missing, massive search efforts began. It wasn't just the rescue squad; the whole town spent two days and two nights looking by land, water and air. There were checkpoints on the border with Portugal, as the authorities speculated that she might have been kidnapped, if she hadn't drowned. At the end of those two days, they found her dead in the pine grove. She was in a spot the police had passed through several times, but it seems that my cousin had got scared and hid. My aunt recounts terrible details she now seems soothed to share with me: when my cousin was found, her fingernails were caked with dirt from digging for moisture. She'd gone thirsty in the heat. Now I remember that my mother did tell me one thing about my cousin: her favourite story, one she ardently loved and demanded to hear every night before bed, was called, 'The Little Girl Who Got Lost in the Woods'. My mother told me this when I was very small, which may be why I've always been afraid of having a favourite story. Perhaps I was spooked that it might attract my death. It's a fear I still have today, but only now does it make sense to me.

I was six years old then. More or less the age I was, give or take, when my mother stopped being able to see me. From then on, it was as if I'd vanished. In my memory, the before and after is perfectly clear, from a loving mother to one who sometimes seemed to despise me. It was her guilt. My aunt says that whenever someone praised me for something, my mother would say, as if to excuse herself, 'But she'll never be like her.'

Adrianne is punctual. Two hours later, she's back. She takes me to a room where a couple of women are seated in two of six chairs arranged in a row. It's a room outfitted for this sole purpose: the hospital dairy farm, the place where women hook their breasts to pumps every few hours, hoping to squeeze out a few drops per session. Adrianne explains how it's done. It's simple.

The process begins with a dull hum as soon as I plug in the machine.

The breast pump is a strange, unsettling contraption designed to extract human milk in an inhuman way. Before I know it, the two clear cones of the machine are already affixed to my nipples, like a lifeless two-mouthed creature suckling at me. My breasts are inflamed again, and they burn, so the suction – which is strong – is very painful. I'm exhausted and suddenly nauseous. This can't be worse than chemotherapy, I think. And if I look, the landscape of my body is grotesque: my nipples are stretched two or three centimetres. I see them because the cones are transparent, a spectacle that could be avoided by making them opaque. I feel captive to this mechanical insect, this domineering figure I've only just met and is already controlling my body.

Once the process is over, Adrianne comes back and assesses my yield. I can't see much, but she shows me a smattering of droplets. 'This is gold for your daughter,' she says. The other mothers glance at me without a word. One looks even more desolate than I feel, and the other has a lot of milk, at least in my view. Lots of gold. Gold that hurts as it must hurt the miners who dig it from the earth.

Then the same hallway again. I return to the armchair beside you. 'You did great,' Adrianne says. 'I'll be back in two hours.' I fall into a deep sleep. When Adrianne wakes me, I'm about to tell her that I don't want the gold. That I can't do it. But the words escape me. I haven't slept for more than two hours at a time for weeks. I find myself plugged in again. My hands shake as I try to fit the cones over my nipples.

This time there's a different woman across from me. 'Try to relax,' she says in a gentle voice. 'If you're nervous or tired, it'll be much harder for your milk to come in.'

Relax, she says. Is she mad? Giving birth to a preemie doesn't mean you can't be crazy, or naive, or an idiot.

There are few humiliations so great as demanding the love of your own mother. I'm pretty sure that only a person who's experienced it will understand. Maybe that's part of why it can't be verbalised. You can't tell a mother the things you'd say to a partner. We can drag ourselves through the dirt for a man or a woman to love us; we can debase ourselves, begging for their love with anguish or without it, and sometimes we do. But nothing compares to the humiliation of the silence when you implore your own mother, speaking in a voice that sounds only in your head: 'I'm your daughter. Love me.' The closest I've gotten, and only once, was when I yelled, 'But why don't you love me?!' I was reading on the sofa; she was sitting in an armchair across from me. At that moment, I felt lucky. My mother had come to New York to be with us, the mood was calm, you were moving around inside me. Here was the mother with whom I thought I might reconcile, or was reconciling, or had reconciled already – because she made an effort to treat me well in those first few days of her visit, and I thought I was willing to forget everything, everything, if she loved you. So I sat there on the sofa, reading, not even reading, just holding the book in my hand, feeling you move around, and thinking about how life had let me open the gift that was right in front of me, years of emptiness all wrapped up with a ribbon: my mother. But she shattered both the moment and my hope, rekindling an old argument out of the blue. *I can't believe this*, I thought. *Here we go again*. It was par for the course with her; she couldn't spend too many days in a state of peace with me, she had to rustle up some drama, and I was always walking on eggshells. Right then, though, I honestly hadn't expected it. I burst into tears, and that's when I cried out, 'But why don't you love me?!'

She didn't answer. She too started to cry, weeping even harder than I was, and stormed out of the flat. It was night-time in New York, a place she didn't know, a city convulsing with isolated episodes of extreme violence prompted by different causes. This was another of her strategies: it wasn't enough for her to hurt me, she needed to make sure I was worried about her. I called her incessantly, but she'd turned off her phone. I went out looking for her, not knowing where to even start. I even called my aunt, her sister, in Spain, in case my mother had reached out. Nothing. Nearly six months pregnant, I walked the city for hours. I couldn't find her. She came home after midnight. I saw her turn on her phone and look at it; the screen lit her face. I'm sure she saw the dozens of missed calls. She'd won my attention yet again.

———

Given the tragic circumstances, when my aunt and uncle arrived from Germany, the airport staff allowed part of the family to meet them right at the doors of the plane. My mother was there, and when my aunt and uncle made their way down the staircase, my Aunt Carmen fainted.

It took twenty years for my aunt to forgive my mother. And even so, I don't think my mother ever forgave me for existing. As if she'd had to choose between the death of her daughter or her niece, and she'd chosen my cousin.

———

The first thing I felt when I got out of the car at the petrol station was a damp trickle down my legs. My two prior miscarriages had started with the same liquid sensation in my inner thighs. The bathroom was locked. I didn't have time to go inside and ask for the key, and I didn't dare try. Without a thought to passers-by, I stuck a hand into my trousers, tugged at my knickers and touched my vagina. The path from the dark of my underwear to the outside world, into my own field of vision, felt endless. When I looked at my finger, it wasn't red, there was no blood, but it was certainly very wet. I remembered something the doctor had said: amniotic fluid smells like bleach. I sniffed, and lo and behold, it smelled a bit like Clorox. As my mother resumed her hysterical crying in the car, I called a taxi to the hospital. My waters had broken. On admission to the hospital, I was four centimetres dilated. It was when they rushed me down the hall on the stretcher that I heard it: 'We're going to try to save them both.'

Today, alone in the pumping room, I turned on the TV for the first time. It's actually a kind of tablet that unfolds from one side of the armchair, like the food tray in an aeroplane. I use headphones, more to isolate myself than to keep from bothering others. There's a news story about a forty-eight-year-old woman who's been murdered in her home in Springfield, Missouri, and her nineteen-year-old daughter has gone missing. The search is urgent, because the girl, born premature, can only get around in a wheelchair, and suffers from muscular dystrophy, leukaemia and asthma. She eats through a feeding tube. If she's still alive, she needs urgent medical attention. But I've missed something; the newsreader then announces that the police are looking for her because she's the primary suspect in her mother's murder. I can't yet put my finger on it, but something about this story speaks to me deeply right now.

When she fled, my mother became an artery unhooked from my heart. The last drops of her blood leave my body through the end of that artery, like the mouth of a garden hose losing strength, thrashing clumsily into stillness.

Ten years ago, I found myself with most of my mother's side of the family in the room where my great-grandmother Dolores was dying. We kissed her, stroked her hands, and thanked her, but she couldn't see or hear us. All she did was cry out for her mother. At nearly one hundred years old, my great-grandmother still needed her mother so she could die. After childbirth, and after the proximity of MyBaby's death, or both of our deaths, I needed my mother too. I thought she'd be able to accompany me this time, and I channelled my wish into a hopeful – if misguided – intuition. But could I love MyChild the same way if I'd been responsible for the death of my niece? I think I could. At the same time, I have no right to say such a thing, and there are moments when I believe I couldn't. My cousin's death was the equator between my mother's love for me and her contempt. The beach. That beach divides the waves of my childhood from the rocks of hell. And to my mother, that beach, that pine grove, is me.

There's no news today about Gypsy-Rose, the girl who allegedly killed her mother. But I've just learned from a brief programme that the Make-A-Wish Foundation, a non-profit devoted to making the wishes of terminally ill children come true, had fulfilled one of Gypsy's wishes some years back: a trip to Disney World. Another organisation, Habitat for Humanity, had built her a pink house (pink is her favourite colour) adapted to her needs, complete with an elegant ramp. I also saw images of Gypsy appearing onstage at a party held to celebrate the Child of the Year awards. She's pale and bald in her wheelchair, but she beams at the camera. There's a teddy bear in her lap. Gypsy has a pink bow on one side of her head and wears a nineteenth-century-style purple flowered dress with a white collar and thick glasses. She's holding a microphone and singing in a high voice. She's out of tune, but it's not the song itself that feels discordant – it's her voice, too shrill and childlike for her age. When she's done singing, her mother thanks the audience and addresses Gypsy to say that she was born to be her mother. Her daughter brings her hands to her face and weeps. At the end of the programme, I learn that Gypsy wasn't twelve, as her mother claimed, but sixteen. No one except her mother, not even Gypsy herself, knew her true age.

The news stories I watched yesterday were out of date, or maybe it's that the Diazepam I was given as an exception – I had a panic attack – put me to sleep before I could get a better sense of the situation. The girl who allegedly killed her mother is now on trial. In the first images I saw, she had no hair. Now she has a full head of healthy locks. She also doesn't need a wheelchair anymore; she walks unassisted, and her voice is deeper, more confident. Gypsy-Rose knows how to defend herself with words.

Chicken in red sauce
Almóndigas
Pisto stew

Cod and tomatoes
Artichokes and ham
Red curry
Menestra stew
Bolognese
Beef tenderloin with mustard
Puchero stew
Chicken tikka masala
Chicken enchiladas (some spicy, some not)
Lasagne

This is the list of recipes I texted to my mother: all the dishes I was cooking so that neither she nor I would have to think about food when we got home from the hospital. I even made sure my handwriting was pretty on the labels I taped to the containers before I froze them. The freezer full of glass dishes gave me a sense of self-sufficiency, of protection, as if I were ready for the city's supermarkets to collapse. I counted them every day, proud and pleased to be caring for my family. Though maybe all this cooking wasn't so much an act of caring for my family as of wanting to create it: through the indivisible alchemy of the ingredients, my mother's tastes and natural attachment to me, mine to my daughter. Maybe cooking was the only way I'd found to build a little world in which, just once, just this once, I could feel like a member of a tribe.

This arsenal of frozen food will be awaiting me when I arrive. I'll have to eat it all myself, or toss some of the dishes I cooked to please my mother's palate alone.

'THAT BITCH IS DEAD!'

'I fucken SLASHED THAT FAT PIG AND RAPED

HER SWEET INNOCENT DAUGHTER ... HER SCREAM WAS SOOOO FUCKEN LOUD LOL.'

That's what appeared on Gypsy's Facebook page, which until then had only shown a girl with cognitive disabilities, childlike and ingenuous for her chronological age, attached to her doting mother and dependent on the charity of different associations and her own neighbours.

Did Gypsy really kill the mother who had apparently renounced all self-interest and lived for nothing but her daughter's welfare? It seems that she did. Not directly, though, but through her boyfriend.

When the ashes of Dee Dee, Gypsy's mother, were delivered to her family, no one wanted to collect them. And when Dee Dee's sister was asked where she'd like to scatter them, she said, 'In the toilet.'

'I'm going to tank you.'

'What do you mean?'

'I'm going to flush you down the toilet and then I'm going to drain the tank.'

I don't know how old I was when I made up this turn of phrase to threaten my mother. And I don't remember why I wanted to tank her.

I must have been around eight. My mother had left for the night shift; my dad and I were home. Before bed, I realised my mother had forgotten her keys on the dining room table. I didn't sleep, just sat on the balcony and waited for her to come back, many hours later, so I could toss her the keys and protect her from my father's wrath. I don't remember her protecting me in the same way.

Gypsy-Rose appears in a video shot on the porch of her pink house. She leaps into the snow. Covered in it, she grabs her legs and starts to drag herself along as if she can't move them. It's the kind of video in which people with physical or psychic challenges experience a moment of joy and thus win the hearts of thousands, even millions of social media followers proclaiming that *x* little boy with hydrocephalus, sustaining a head too large to hold up by himself, is the most beautiful thing they've ever seen, or that *y* little girl, whose tumour makes her face look melted into dangling layers of skin, should be a model. And no one tells them to fuck off. Nor does anyone actually show any interest in them except for the spectators, who are little more than a virtual version of those old circuses exhibiting and exploiting a three-breasted woman or a dwarf covered in hair. Gypsy too went unnoticed to everyone but the voyeurs of other people's deformities.

Gypsy's medical reports assert the following conditions, which her mother attributes to the girl's premature birth: epilepsy, vision problems, cognitive delays (mental age: seven), acid reflux, quadriplegia, hearing problems, muscular dystrophy, anaemia, hyperventilation, allergies, leukaemia (since the age of five), incontinence, lung disease and a heart murmur.

But Gypsy is a perfectly healthy young woman.

Since everyone believed, as her mother insisted, that

Gypsy was mentally seven years old, no one ever considered her opinions or pleas for help. Abandoned by her doctors, relatives, friends and an entire social service and child protection system, Gypsy found no way to escape her systematic confinement and abuse other than to end her mother's life. She felt free in prison. She started to gain weight. She began to walk and eat like almost everyone else: through her mouth. Her feeding tube was removed forever. Her mother had invented all of her ailments as a form of control, and Gypsy herself had learned to believe them since she was very small. In prison, Gypsy perceived the colour and waves of her own hair: no one was shaving her head anymore.

What's the difference between the suffering caused by a mother who tortures her daughter to keep her from growing up, to ensure that she'll always be able to take care of her, and the suffering caused by a mother with a daughter she always viewed as an adult, or as altogether non-existent? At least Gypsy knows it, says it to the cameras: her mother loved her. She knows that her mother, mired in her own illness and madness, did love her. That's more than I can say of mine.

When my mother left me alone, I lived for a while in a house where the front door didn't properly open or shut. To go in, all you had to do was lift it slightly and push. It wasn't all bad: while my grandparents incubated their grown-up chick, my friends took me under their wings, nurtured me under the warmth of their teenage feathers. Sometimes up to four of us would sleep in my little bed. But when all was said and done, on holidays, birthdays, or simply the routine of one meal after another, I was on my own. If I didn't make it home one night, no one would come looking for me for several days. And once they did, the first person to search was never my own flesh and blood.

In many ways, things got better. But once you've known such piercing loneliness, it becomes chronic, takes up all the space (outside, inside), relegates us to a box in the furthest corner of our own bodies. Sometimes I think I gestated MyChild with the same blueprint used to build a room, the same materials used to make a nest. Spit and clay, like a swallow. Maybe motherhood was the only way I found to have a home that no one could evict me from.

I remember a day when I felt overwhelmed by what I lacked. I went out and sat down on the first stoop I saw. I started to cry, helplessly, as if no one could see me (could anyone see me?). A woman walking down the street stopped short, reached for my hands, helped me up, and hugged me fiercely, pressing my chest hard to hers. And then she walked away. She didn't say a word, but the syntax was complete; I've never forgotten it. No one had ever offered me such real, direct solace as that total stranger.

My place in Seville had seven balconies. It wasn't a luxury flat; it was just that the architect had taken pains to design something modest but aesthetically pleasing. My parents had bought it as a low-income housing unit in a neighbourhood, La Alameda, that was still known as a major red-light district. I can say I went to a good school because I learned a lot on the way. It was a half-hour walk. Some ageing prostitutes still sat around chatting in their wood or wicker chairs. I realised that pubic hair starts falling out at a certain age, which is why they painted theirs on. If I could time-travel, I'd visit their homes to inform them that laser hair removal is par for the course now. Actually, no. I'd visit them and say: Thank you for smiling at me as if you didn't already bear the burden of so many despicable men. But as I was saying, my house had seven balconies, each with red carnations and geraniums. On the corner there was an open-air cinema, the Cine Ideal, whose movie dialogues echoed down the street on sultry summer nights, and whose screen I could see if I went up onto the roof. That's when I started watching films. I wasn't yet thirteen, walking home from school, when a man first pulled over in his car and asked how much I charged. Many more would follow, but I got used to it, because my flat had seven balconies and an open-air cinema on the corner, and besides, right across from my bedroom window was an ancient tower, inscriptions and all: Prince Don Fadrique's tower, a damp, abandoned thirteenth-century construction. In the morning, I got to stare out at the scenes on other rooftops, with clothes hung up to dry like white goats. But the tower grew imposing by night. On some days, my mother, when she was still taking care of me, still able to acknowledge my material presence, came up to the roof to find me, and we'd take the five-minute walk to the tower and go in, seeking refuge in the deserted, tumbledown old building. I'd explore every nook and cranny as if trying to locate the sores on a stray dog. No one tended to the tower back then. There were thick chains hanging from one of the walls by the entrance. No one denied – because no one was there – that Frederick of Castile had been tortured there for loving the wrong woman. I'd climb the stairs with my mother, our presence equally disruptive to cats and rats, and I'd be panting with excitement, knowing that another rooftop awaited me at the end, a battlemented one, from which I could see my own. My gasps echoed in the belly of the tower, and it was as if all the mothers, daughters, cats, rats, towers and princes of a distant past were breathing to the same rhythm. No one barred our ascent as I peered through the tiny windows and trained my eyes on the ancient bird that Don Fadrique surely envied during his confinement. There was no one around to tell him that a little girl was admiring him from a future century. And after the stairs came the best part of all: a kind of tall, thin trunk with rungs like cut boughs that let us keep climbing sunward. I went first as my mother held my feet. The whole mast shuddered, but I wasn't afraid: ships move, reeds move, the spine moves, and there was no security guard in sight to impose silly precautions. The guard came later: I saw him on my first visit back home in 2016, after many years away. The city had implemented a conservation plan for the tower: the extermination of rats and cats, fixed hours, guided tours, the guide's speech I didn't want to hear. Because as far as I was concerned, the tower was my tower, as long as there was no one to speak for it, to insist on explaining, as if stones can't explain themselves. The guide snuffed the light in my tower: the glow that had been my night light for so many childhood years, illuminating my bedroom.

My mother can't understand that the only sense of belonging I feel when I think of home is in a wardrobe at her house. That's where I store clothes, shoes and mementos from when I was small, things I obviously don't want to take with me as I move from rented flat to rented flat: hundreds of letters, dating back to when I was nine or ten years old and my diaries too. It's packed with things of mine, things that take up space. My mother has gone on for years about how my possessions get in her way. A single wardrobe in a whole house. I dream of getting it all out of there, getting my own place, making a home with my daughter. But it does hurt that my mother wants to discard the only piece of furniture that symbolises family for me, a sense of belonging in her home: a simple wardrobe.

Maybe there should be an organisation like Habitat for Humanity that provides little storage units, even underground containers, where those of us who've never felt at home in our families can keep our things, our memories – because I'm afraid of removing them from my mother's wardrobe. What if they get lost? That's another problem. I don't want to lose all my memories if I open the wardrobe, take everything out and haul it across the Atlantic with me. That wardrobe contains things I don't have in my head, things my head can't remember by itself, because it doesn't want to. Which is why I wish that someone – my mother, in this case – not only wouldn't reject them, but would take care of them for me. An impossible task.

I'd never had these sorts of nightmares until the bottle cap incident, but now they're recurring: I beat my mother. The motives for my hatred are strange. I hit her because she doesn't love me. Can you hate someone for not loving you? If a mother's un-love hurts, it's because you love her. So how can you hate her? That's how I discovered this peculiar form of hate, like antibiotic-resistant hospital bacteria, something I'd never felt until now, hate in its worst form, the most lethal for both transmitter and receiver: the hate that springs from love.

These nightmares feature the scene I've recounted, the one that actually happened. Always, invariably, in every single nightmare, is our drive back from the beach. My mother at the wheel. The argument she forced. She always wins through drama. That's her strategy. She thinks she can turn reality in her favour by screaming and crying. The bottlecap. Coughing as if she were choking. The motorway. My panic. The petrol station. My waters breaking nearly four months before my due date. The taxi. The hospital. The *We're going to try to save them both.* The abandonment.

Dee Dee and Gypsy-Rose moved to Aurora, Missouri, in 2005, after Hurricane Katrina destroyed their flat in Louisiana. They quickly became two of the best-known and most beloved members of the community. Who could resist a single mother who'd sacrificed everything, down to the merest personal ambition or wish, to care round the clock for a daughter with such varied and overwhelming needs – and had done so, moreover, with such a sense of gratitude? Because, as Dee Dee often said, it was the depth of her daughter's love that sustained her. Such humility, such selflessness in the face of her own will and wellbeing. The very purest form of love.

They rented a place until Habitat for Humanity finished building their pink house, complete with a special ramp for Gypsy. They started over in a community that admired them. Dee Dee only lamented that the flooding in Louisiana had done away with, among so many other things, her daughter's medical records. In Missouri, the doctors continued to treat Gypsy as Dee Dee insisted she needed. They changed her feeding tube periodically, prescribed dozens of pills to keep from interrupting her previous regimen. When the police entered Dee Dee's home, they found an enormous wardrobe filled with medications of all kinds: jars by the hundreds, boxes, syrups. A wardrobe far larger than my mother's. Why do I have to envy a little girl who was a victim? Why do I find myself comparing us based on our mothers' attention and care? Why do I feel tenderly towards Dee Dee for the very same reasons that led her daughter to kill her? It all seems relative; everything is, really. I need some form of assurance. Maybe if I were given a firm, solemn, military order, I'd follow it, if only in hopes that justice could be done:

Forgive your mother!

I'd forgive her.

Don't forgive her!

Then I'd never forgive her.

Is that how fragile I am?

Gypsy's mother had her undergo an unnecessary operation to extract her salivary glands. She also had almost all of her teeth pulled; at the age of sixteen, Gypsy was already using dentures. At night – and during much of the day as well – Dee Dee administered her narcotics through a feeding tube, so Gypsy always seemed to be floating about in another world, detached from reality, babbling, her head listing to one side as she sat in her wheelchair. Of course she appeared to be disabled. But the truth unknown to everyone else is that Gypsy-Rose was simply drugged.

After having spent half my life in another country (or better put, after having had to spend half my life in another country), I started to forget certain aspects of Seville, my home city. I didn't even notice at first. Once I did, it felt like a tragedy. You never lose your birthplace, but if you don't return once in a while, you need to learn to walk all over again: to recognise the sound of your footsteps, the feel of the living room sofa, tender as a childhood toy. When I travel to Spain after a long time and must relearn how to change the gas tank at the flat, or when, in the neighbourhood where I grew up, someone asks me where my accent is from, I imagine a doctor telling a patient, 'You're losing your city's cerebral response.' Then I look down at my arms and seek the path that connects me to the IV drip, so I can pull it out, and reply: 'Doctor, who do you think you are? My city is here, I feel it. It's pulsing in me.'

But it's not so easy.

Seville. The last time I went, I no longer knew how to walk around it. I lost my way in places I'd been to many times. When I tried to take the route from my long-lost flat to the conservatory where I studied piano for eight years – a ten-minute walk at most – I hesitated. Wept. How could this be? I thought my city would await me forever. When did it happen, the point of no return? How soon would I have had to come back for the map to remain unaltered in my memory? I felt like an Andalusian dog from nowhere. Not going home is like spending a long time without looking in the mirror: your face won't vanish, and your personality won't either, but when you glance at yourself again, everything seems new and unreachably remote. Everything about you seems to belong to someone else. That's the problem: what you don't recognise is in you, everywhere, it's in the lengths and joints of your bones, it *is* you, but at the same time you don't feel like what you are.

My mother has hurt me countless times. If she could simply acknowledge this, that might be enough for me. But whenever I've asked her to do so, she's risen up as a victim. That's the verb I want: she rises up. She raises her voice, and she herself grows taller, straighter, cranking up the volume of her sobs, which somehow are never as heart-rending as she intends; she rehearses too much for her tears to be persuasive. My mother will never comfort me by recognising what she's done in the past. I need to stop asking her. It makes less and less sense over time, and her reactions only become more hollow and more hysterical. The last time I confronted her, her response was unprecedented: 'Your father beat me up whenever I did or said something he didn't like, and then I'd do the same thing a few days later, knowing he'd beat me up again. It's like that when I hurt you. I can't help it.'

Of course, Mama, but I've never hit you. I'm the one who bears the blows inside me.

Now that I know more about what happened on the beach in Huelva, I feel the urge to call her and say something like: I know. You think you killed my cousin. I don't believe you killed her, but you were still responsible for her death. She was three years old and her mother was the last person to see her body. She'd already gotten the news by the time she flew back. A flight bound for death. This was many years ago. My aunt forgave you. Be good to my daughter. Love her and I'll forgive you for everything. I'll forgive you so wholly that I'd let you take her to the beach alone. To the very same beach in Huelva. To the pine grove there. That's my only condition: love her.

A few days ago, my friend Claudia shared a story I found so powerful that her off-handedness surprised me; she told it as if it were any ordinary anecdote. In this recollection of her childhood, I heard echoes of my own. It went more or less like this:

> I was the tallest kid in my class at school. I developed early and was about as tall as I am now, so I felt a bit distant from the others and fantasised about fitting in better. One day a cockroach appeared in the classroom and a boy picked it up. Everyone clapped and praised him for daring to grab it in his own hands. After that, I spent a long time begging silently for another cockroach, so that I could be the one to catch it and receive my classmates' admiration. I waited for a long time. Finally, one afternoon, a dead cockroach turned up. I hurried to collect it, held it up by the wings, and displayed my achievement to the whole class. They insulted me and called me nasty.

That's what part of my childhood was like: I spent it hunting for cockroaches so that my mother would notice I was there. But it didn't work.

I have almost entirely happy memories of my mother before she turned thirty-two. But that age is engraved in my mind, because that's when I started to weigh her down. I was six or seven at the time, so I couldn't know that the burden wasn't me, but my little cousin's dirt-caked fingernails. The torches of a whole town searching for her at night. Heavy food in the stomach after swimming in the sea. Sluggishly digesting. It's as if that was when I became an adult to my mother. From then on, I would have to take care of myself.

MyChild, look, here: I've brought you something I wrote when I was little and lovingly kept for you ever since. I wrote it with my mother. I was thinking of having it framed to hang up in your room, next to your first letter to the Three Kings. In my own first letter, I asked for three presents:

An enormous acorn.

Chestnuts you can eat.

A tree that's a little bit big and a little bit small.

The first thing that stands out to me is that I didn't ask for toys (you'll have lots of those waiting for you). I suppose I'd already developed a special penchant for food (you'll soon experience that pleasure too). Especially foods I was used to collecting in the countryside:

Enormous acorns: as far as I can remember, the larger they were, the juicier their meat.

Chestnuts you can eat: because many of the ones I gathered had worms in them. I'd split the chestnut in half with my teeth, and there it was, a tiny worm, white and writhing. That's the explanation found by my now-self, my adult self, for why I said so specifically that they had to be chestnuts 'you can eat.'

As for the tree 'that's a little bit big and a little bit small,' I imagine this was my way of requesting a medium-sized tree, neither big nor small; one I could climb easily, but which wouldn't cause me any serious harm if I fell.

There's a fig tree growing in the tiny yard behind our flat. Its branches await you.

When I was young, I made a faint cut across the veins of my wrist and pressed my blood to the blood of my best friend, who had done the same. Startled by how freely the blood flowed from that part of my body, I realised why it's a common method of suicide. This friend is still in my life today. It was a symbolic act that didn't force us into some lifelong pact of friendship; we've honoured it happily, with care, with a sense of humour. It was an offering.

I feel like my mother has broken a blood oath. I didn't receive the full force of her betrayal when she hurt me before I became a mother, but now, with her indifference towards you, I do; she's broken a blood oath that I'd never break with a friend. I no longer believe in the power of genetic blood, and yet I want to believe, because it's another of the ties that bind me to you. Because it has to be, I want it to be. My mother has revealed the second universal lie: the potency and preciousness of daughterly blood. The first lie is the belief that the Three Kings exist, although of course that one's entirely forgivable.

I still believe in the night of the fifth of January; I still keep that illusion alive. But the blood-lie, the cavalcade that connects mothers and children, mothers and grandchildren, is gone. The Three Kings exist, even if they don't. A mother's blood doesn't exist, even if it does.

Mama, do you know why I get my period every month?

Tell me.

To rid myself of your blood, bit by bit.

Don't you love me?

I don't know anymore. In any case, if I love you, it won't be because you're my mother, but in spite of that.

When I started to notice that my mother was pushing me away, I also started asking her questions to test how much she loved me. Most of the time she'd say whatever I wanted to hear in a sweet voice, which is obviously what I was angling for. And so my questions got more extreme. I wanted to guarantee that my mother loved me more than absolutely anything else in the world. And so, naturally, I ended up formulating a question with an answer that caused me pain:

'Would you kill all the birds in the world for me?'

'All the birds in the world? No.'

In spite of everything, my mother was present, in some way or another, until I was fourteen, when she left. Then she turned up a couple years later, introducing herself as a friend. And as a friend, she was the kind you can sometimes count on but mostly can't. For a long time, I didn't feel that she came up short emotionally. We lived many miles away, but I went to visit her with some regularity, and it was fun. That was the word. I felt fine about my fun friend.

At thirty-two, then, my mother was my friend, but at sixty she decided to become my enemy. She grew embittered, mired herself in family feuds, complicated every conversation and began to judge any decision I made. This phase overlapped with my struggle to get pregnant, which made it all even more painful for me. My inability to give her a grandchild seemed to dash any hope that some tendril of her being would reach towards me again, springing up green and fresh. On the other hand, she seemed thoroughly uninterested in having a grandchild at all. Each of us strained at either end of the rope pulled taut between us. Me, so she would love me; her, to prove that she didn't need to. As I understand it now, she buried her maternal instinct on that beach, couldn't stomach the intensity of my own, and so she belittled my suffering, as if my need to have a child were a kind of self-inflicted wound. I think of the so-called grandmother hypothesis, which seeks to explain the fact that only the females of a small number of species (that is, humans and some cetaceans) far outlive their evolutionary function; in other words, far past menopause, which is rare in biology, even among mammals more like human beings. Most species live only as long as they're able to reproduce. This hypothesis suggests that women live long past menopause in order to continue their reproductive function and preserve their DNA in another form: by helping their children raise their grandchildren. Which makes it essential, evolutionarily speaking, for grandmothers to want to have grandchildren, and to love them.

I remember many of my mother's grievances; she's a walking complaint. She can't, doesn't know how, doesn't want to face the world through any other language. She wants pity; it's her way of staying the centre of attention. I think she wants to be my cousin. She wants the world to mourn her, because no amount of mourning will ever be enough for her to forget what happened: the life that slipped out of her arms because she was careless enough to fall asleep. I've long had terrible thoughts I tried to drive away, but I don't want to silence them anymore: maybe my mother needed my father's violence so she could survive the memory of that beach. In truth, my mother needed my lunatic of a father for many years after their separation. She needed him so she could compare me to him and try to hurt me: 'You're just like your father,' she'd say. I know it's not true, but it's still painful. My mother still needs my father so she can hit me, and so she can hit herself.

When I was a child, on the days my mother burned the lentils, which was often, my father would fling the dish against the wall. I'd stay frozen at the table and say, as if nothing at all had happened, 'I think the lentils taste great.' They were actually inedible, but I'd force them down to ease my father's rage. I learned not to react when the plate struck. Sometimes I imagine that if I ever experience an earthquake, I'll be able to keep entirely still through the tremors. That's how fine my seismic training was. I'm a fundamentally decent person, but when my mother left this hospital and I swelled with fury against her, I could no longer be sure that I'd defend her at all costs. I don't think I'd be able to swallow her burned lentils today. Maybe I'd have tossed them against the wall myself. Violence is never justified, blah blah blah. But leaving your daughter who's just given birth with her life still at risk and your one-point-one-pound granddaughter confined to an incubator – that's violence too. Leaving, just like that, without so much as a phone call.

Latin can be so ridiculous. Accustomed as I am to its use as a mark of erudition, the exercise of a lettered few, or a form of nostalgia for a long-lost mother tongue, I occasionally find a Latin etymology of certain words that takes them down a notch, makes them smaller and humbler. For instance, the word 'lens' comes from the Latin 'lentil'. It seems that someone once noticed the similarity between the curve of a lens and that of the seed.

My interest in nutrition has led me, both deliberately and by accident, beyond the nutritional value of each ingredient. And so I know that the cultivation of lentils dates back to the Neolithic period, and they're hardy enough to weather drought and thrive in diverse terrain.

Their high iron content makes them especially beneficial in pregnancy. When I cooked them over the months, I'd often freeze some to increase my postpartum food supply. What's more, their high fibre content makes them a useful digestive aid – another boon for a pregnant person. A smooth, good-sized shit is downright priceless when you feel so heavy you can't tell the difference between the foetus and your own waste.

Most importantly of all: grandmothers cook lentils. Always. As I cooked, I'd think about how my mother was about to become a grandmother. She'd like the lentils. When the time came to unfreeze them, I'd simply have to make a bit of rice, add it to the plate and voilà: a complete protein source.

Some of my mother's complaints were recurrent, like an allergy to a plant we couldn't identify, and came without rhyme or reason. She practically sneezed out her grievances. Here's one: 'When I gave birth to you, your grandmother put me in the bed where Laika had given birth just a few days before.'

Laika was the dog of my early childhood, a German shepherd who never left my side. And by 'your grandmother', my mother meant my father's mother.

This complaint, which no one else believed was real, persisted for years. She'd sneeze it out here and there. If I had to sneeze out everything she regarded with contempt, I'd never have time to breathe. I'd hyperventilate until I fainted.

My friends did protect me, and so did their mothers. Getting to know them was my good fortune and my hardship. They weren't like mine. They were mothers. That's the only way to put it: mothers. Mine wasn't one. My friends always said that my mother was like a friend. They meant it as a good thing, but it horrified me. When the mother of one of my best friends died young, I thought the wrong mother had gone. Maybe I would have grieved my mother's death as bitterly as my friend grieved hers, but it would have been a very different pain: she mourned because her mother had always been there, while I would have mourned because mine no longer had the chance to. Not even once.

It felt like a long fish fluttering in my belly. Just for a couple of seconds. Impossible. I'd been told it was too soon to feel you moving. But the next day it happened again, twice. And on the third day I knew for sure: it was you.

When I found out I was pregnant, I felt an urgent need to ask my mother what I was like as a child. I had lots of other questions too: When would the nausea stop? Had I moved around a lot when she was pregnant with me? She didn't remember anything, except for one thing she was very confident about: I never moved, she said, or else she never felt me. For nine months. She never felt me.

I think she did. She must have felt me, there's no way she didn't, but maybe she pushed me away, even out of her dreams. It's been proven that one of the functions of dreaming is to reinforce what we've learned while we're awake. Without dreaming, we forget. My mother's dreams were left behind on the sand, out at sea, stuck to the resin on the pines of Huelva.

On one of my first nights in the hospital, ignoring the doctor's advice, I gathered all my cables, tried not to get tangled up in them, got out of bed and went to the bathroom. I looked into the mirror, expecting to find – and I wouldn't have cared if I had – an unrecognisable version of myself. But there I was, the shape of my body less altered than I'd imagined. My curves hadn't yet been erased, my belly still bulged a bit. Hips covered in a disposable nappy, swollen breasts cupped in a nursing bra, I couldn't help but feel like the wounded animal I was. But I also felt beautiful. That was a surprise, a tiny gift that softened those sordid hours. With great effort, I hobbled back into the room, found my bag and fished out my phone and lipstick. I returned to the bathroom and took a selfie in the enormous mirror. It was true: I looked good, beautiful, strong, more alive than dead. Much more. When my mother came to visit, I showed her the photo. Her reaction hit me like a wave against the coast: 'What a tasteless picture. And very unflattering. Delete it.'

There she was again – my mother underscoring, or in this case inventing, my flaws. Even if she didn't think I looked pretty in the photo, a lie would have been healing to me. But my mother only lies when the truth would make you feel better. I was still in bad shape; the photo could have been my last, and she knew it.

I remember a strange episode, though strange is an understatement. When my mother's first post-divorce boyfriend decided to leave her, she spent the next few months trying to exert extreme forms of control over me. It didn't last long, and at first I took it as a sign that she needed my company. But I was twenty years old by then. I'd been abandoned a long time ago, and I didn't know – didn't want to know – how to live without freedom, how to deal with a mother who'd never restricted my comings and goings and was now trying to keep me under curfew as a legal adult. Then she started threatening suicide whenever I hadn't called her for a while, or when I visited and left earlier than she hoped. On one of those days, expecting to hear her threats of self-annihilation as soon as I shut the door behind me, I left her a note on the dining room table:

> Mama, in case you decide to kill yourself, I'm leaving you these three things:
>
> A knife
> Bleach
> Pills
>
> I'd recommend the pills. I'm pretty sure the other methods are more painful.

I left in tears. But I left.

My mother had lots of boyfriends, nearly all of them toxic. Now I understand that this may have been her way of setting the clock of her life on I-don't-deserve-to-live mode. Only the first was a teenager, but they were all much younger than her. There's nothing inherently wrong with that, but it does say something about my mother's underlying drive to abandonment. After all, this is a society in which, despite occasional efforts to argue the contrary, young men invariably leave older women. Although she always did like married men of all ages. I only got along with two of her boyfriends: the first, who was Romanian, and one of the last, a guy from Córdoba, in Spain. I was fifteen when my mother was dating the Romanian. He'd take me to department stores to shoplift clothes and luxury items he later resold. Normally they were commissions, that is, some friend or regular client would see something they liked and ask him for it. Then we'd go and steal it, employing techniques I found astoundingly clever. He always treated me with warmth and kindness, and I enjoyed participating in a kind of criminal behaviour that couldn't really incriminate me, since I was a minor. We'd shoplift in Puerto Banús, a marina with enormous yachts, underage girls on the arms of Russian millionaires, window displays flaunting two-thousand-euro bras. To borrow from the Spanish saying, I had the sense that robbing a thief comes with a hundred years of forgiveness. I still do, but that's another story.

My mother's second-to-last boyfriend was an alcoholic. One day, I can't remember why, he punched a hole in the bathroom door; the repair is still visible if you look closely. We clashed at first, but then I warmed up to him. He was an alcoholic, sure, but he was nice to me, and sincere; whatever he said, I could always be confident he wasn't lying. My mother never drank, but she lied more than she spoke. A straightforward example: whenever she saw me after we hadn't met up for a while, she'd say, 'You look nice, you're very pretty today.' Six months later, she'd see me again and say, 'You look really nice, very pretty today. The last time you looked awful.' And so on and so forth. Always. I could never trust her, not even in the smallest of ways.

When I told my mother that Alex, another boyfriend, was cheating on her, which I knew because we frequented the same clubs and I'd seen him making out with other women, she slapped me. Then she burst into tears and started screaming, accusing me of being a liar. Then she got into bed. The room was dark, but there was enough light for me to see how quickly her whole head of hair went damp from sweat, from stress, from her hatred of me or him or both. She yelled the most terrible things at me. Denied it all.

For months, maybe even a year, my mother still dismissed me as a liar – until a doctor diagnosed her with a sexually transmitted disease that only her boyfriend could have given her. It was her own afflicted vagina that proved me right in my mother's eyes.

My few surviving childhood photos are in the wardrobe at my mother's house, the one that bothers her so much. I was five months pregnant, holidaying in Spain, when we got into an argument. My mother opened the wardrobe door, grabbed all the photos in a rage and flung them into the air. I felt so unloved, so defenceless, so despised once again, that I too seized the closest thing on hand – the printer – and hurled it to the floor as hard as I could. Then I locked myself in the bathroom, sat down on the floor with my back to the door and burst into uncontrollable tears. My mother left when she heard me, didn't offer so much as a word of solace. I immediately went and found my handheld doppler, laid down in bed and listened for MyChild's heartbeat. It was fast. I felt guilty, relieved that my mother had left the house. At that moment, I hated her, hated her for making my daughter suffer through me.

My mother didn't come back for two days. When

she did, she was in victim-mode: she'd had to sleep on the beach, she said. I didn't yet know what the beach meant to her. I might have hugged her if I'd known. But do I even remember how to hug my mother? It's been so many years since we last embraced that the very thought makes me feel shy, uncomfortable. The idea of hugging my mother strikes me as almost incestuous, or maybe that's not quite the right word, but it feels like invading the blood of a blood relation who neither wants nor deserves invasion. Hugging my mother, even now, feels like committing a crime. I'd rather shoplift.

It's the second time I've ever been hospitalised. The first was for a serious case of pneumonia. The doctors advised me to call my family. I phoned my mother. She was at my grandparents' house. She thought she'd hung up when I heard her say: 'She's in the hospital with pneumonia, she says. What does she expect me to do from here? If she dies, they'll call me.'

I must have been about twenty-two. I was already living in the US. I'd just had my first panic attack and called a friend from university because I didn't understand what was happening. I remember I was so anxious that my teeth hurt. My friend instantly figured it out and told me to wait at my flat; he'd come and spend the evening with me. We talked, he helped distract me, we watched a movie, I calmed down. A huge snowstorm was forecast that night, the kind of blizzard that shuts down the campus for a week and prompts people to stock up on days' worth of food before hunkering down. The supermarkets get completely cleaned out. I asked my friend to stay over, as driving back to his place would be extremely dangerous in those conditions. But since he lived on the far end of Long Island, he decided to leave and wait out the storm at home. He left. I slept soundly.

Two months went by. One day after class, I asked my friend for a ride home. When we reached the parking lot, I saw he had a different car. I asked what had happened to the other one; a used car, perfectly decent, ideal for a student's basic needs. That's when I learned that my friend had had an accident on the day of the blizzard. He was unharmed, but the car was completely wrecked and he'd had to buy another one. He hadn't said anything so I wouldn't feel responsible, and to keep my anxieties at bay in a season of such harsh internal weather for me. That day, at the age of twenty-two, I learned what a mother's warmth and protection must feel like.

Since I'd miscarried several times, I waited to share the news of my pregnancy. First I waited the usual three months that so many women live by, to keep themselves and other people from getting their hopes up. But when the three months had passed, I decided to safeguard my secret until the five-month scan, and then I kept waiting out of fear, withholding the news from friends and relatives. Finally, when MyChild came early, I figured there were still some people who didn't know I was pregnant. To my surprise, everyone knew. In fact, my mother had shared photos of me pregnant in a bikini, even though I'd wanted to keep it private. But she's always decided whether or not my feelings are unreasonable. If they don't match her own, they're unreasonable, which gives her the right to hurt me: 'Don't be stupid. It makes no sense to hide it. If you lose it, you lose it, but you're too far along for that now.'

She always gets to decide. That's why she hasn't known much about me for years: years in which I've not only mistrusted her, but excluded her from feelings and experiences I would have sooner shared with perfect strangers.

When my mother posted those photos, taken in the most vulnerable time of my life, she included a caption, the one she uses whenever she wants to keep me from something that's mine and mine alone: 'Don't tell Marina I told you.'

My mother has a dog. He's a lab/pitbull mix, large, strong, beautiful, great with people, very aggressive with other dogs. A few months ago, we took him out for a walk, and my mother carried the bag she'd just used to pick up one of his enormous excrements. Another dog walked by, and my mother's dog went wild, broke free of his leash, lunged to attack. Not knowing what to do, my mother started hitting her dog with the bag of shit, which broke and scattered its content through the air and onto the bodies of everyone placidly drinking their coffee on the nearby terrace with an ocean view.

Good things about my mother: until my cousin's death, she was always kind, lively, affectionate. She'd sing to me, tickle me, fill my head with all the little birds a child's head needs. She was tremendously imaginative, dynamic, athletic. And she loved me.

I must have been about ten years old. My mother often masturbated while we watched TV, slipping her hand into her pyjamas. I was witness to the movements she tried, though not very hard, to hide it. I wasn't quite sure what she was doing, but these scenes came flooding back to me when I finally learned what masturbation was. I don't feel the need to understand why she didn't do it in her own room, and I don't feel this need because I don't believe she was actually seeing me at all. Could she be blamed for masturbating in front of a daughter she didn't see?

Maybe it's a coincidence, but one of the first movies my mother shared with me was *The Invisible Man*, the original James Whale production from 1933. I was especially struck by the scene in which the invisible man, the scientist Jack Griffin, whose face is covered in bandages, confronts the policemen who have come to arrest him for failing to pay his rent. In that moment, Griffin uncovers his face, and every bandage he removes turns into nothing, into air: his face disappears, his eyes disappear, his entire face disappears until only a headless body remains. Terrified by what they've witnessed, the policemen flee and Griffin strips down, becoming completely transparent.

Maybe my mother wrapped me in so many bandages that when they fell off or I removed them myself, she stopped seeing me altogether.

I didn't know what it really meant to make a decision until the doctors thrust MyChild's fate into my hands. Today they inform me that she needs a blood transfusion, but also that transfusions in twenty-seven-week babies are high-risk. If I approve the procedure, I need to sign a consent form. The doctors don't take decisions on my behalf because they themselves don't know what's best, but sometimes I feel like I'm signing off on how I want my daughter to die. It's A or B in this case, although other decisions involve more letters of the alphabet.

One doctor says that transfusions are necessary for preemies because their bodies haven't had enough time to finish developing the organs and systems that permit the production of red blood cells. As a result, MyBaby's haemoglobin levels are low, which means her body isn't being sufficiently oxygenated and puts her life in serious peril. Blood transfusions are common in such cases, and the way I translate this for myself is: if I decide to consent, it won't be her last transfusion. This doctor – he's new to me – rations information as if from an eyedropper, but I get what he means: when he says 'transfusion', he really means 'transfusions' in the plural. And I also know that he knows I know; he can tell I'm not oblivious to how methodically he doles out the details. As if it hurts less that way. Or maybe it does hurt less, not because it makes much of a difference to receive more or less information all at once, but because I can see he's trying to take care not only of MyChild but also of my feelings, for which I'm grateful.

But an eyedropper is an eyedropper, and I need to know the risks of blood transfusion at twenty-seven weeks:

Transfusion reactions, primarily due to an immature immune system. These reactions may be mild, like fever and hives, or severe, like anaphylactic shock.

Potentially deadly infections.

Fluid overload, due to the immaturity of the kidneys and other organs. A blood transfusion may increase blood volume and therefore elevate the risk of excess fluid.

A blood transfusion may also increase the risk of acute respiratory distress syndrome, which could permanently damage her lungs.

Due to her low platelet levels and other blood-related factors, MyChild may be prone to blood clotting disorders.

And now, with this information in hand, I need to choose all by myself. A or B. And fast. MyChild needs blood. OK. I choose A: transfusion.

I sign without reading what I'm signing.

A nurse comes in. To avoid inserting an IV needle, given how tiny and frail her veins are, the nurse pricks her heel with a lancet to obtain a small blood sample and check her haemoglobin levels before the transfusion. She leaves. Comes back. She asks another nurse to hold down my daughter. She inserts a needle of miniscule diameter into the umbilical vein. 'This is a good vein because it's large and close to the heart,' she tells me.

I've chosen A. I hadn't even noticed the blood in the bag, rippling like a flag without a country or a people. MyChild suddenly looks even paler. Have I made the right decision? Then she starts to take on a pinker, healthier hue. Her breathing deepens, as if she were relaxing before sleep. Yes, it looks like I have. For now. That's all I can aspire to.

The blood flows through her minuscule veins, carrying along a promise of life renewed for another spell. But with every heartbeat, every surge of vital liquid, she's at greater risk of fluid overload. A burden too great for MyBaby's small, vulnerable body to bear.

Her fine, fragile veins baulk at the rush of blood they've just received, and liquid accumulates slowly but persistently in her tissues. I can see MyChild's delicate, translucent skin go taut, as if the blood's force were pressing it to the limit.

Every breath grows heavier and more strained, and her tiny body struggles for balance between life and death. In an instant, fluid overload can cause lung failure, brain damage and other unexpected hazards.

Confronted with these obvious signs of inflammation, the nurse calls for the doctors, and they rush to ease the burden on my daughter's body, reduce the amount of fluid in her system. But time is a fearsome enemy, and my baby teeters on the edge of life.

I choose B. I choose B. But it's too late. And maybe that wouldn't have been the right choice either.

I've heard it repeatedly. The nurses have said it to other mothers here: *Your child will tell you, in some way you're able to understand, that it's time to say goodbye*. I've been in this hospital for so long that I know what hell is. We mothers tend to wonder if we're just prolonging the suffering of our children, if they're going to die regardless. We have to decide, without any kind of medical training, if we'd rather have our baby's body cut open in some new procedure they're unlikely to survive, or if we'd rather face the consequences of not operating. Which means letting the baby go in our arms. Unplugging the cables and embracing them, free at last. Letting them rest. But it's not that easy. I've seen mothers decide to interrupt their agony forever and then spend days holding their child. Days in which their child keeps living without any form of medical assistance. Days in which, minute by minute, they've begged for their child to die, for their decision to be validated. I don't want to end up like that, which is why I've always opted for the suffering of MyChild. Open her up, pump her up, resuscitate her, invade her with IVs, as if she were a voodoo doll stuck with pins, anything – just don't put her in my arms for me to watch her die and then watch her not dying for days, not dying, not dying, until she does, until she arrives so late to her own death that I spend the rest of my life wondering if I should have let her die in the operating room.

I cling to historical facts, any I can find. Paul Denucé, a Belgian doctor in the nineteenth century, had the idea for what would become the first incubator by observing nature – or, better put, by observing a controlled form of nature. One day, visiting a farm, he watched some hens brooding their eggs in a safe and studied environment. People have known since time immemorial that premature babies need an essential kind of support: heat. Mothers would wrap their babies in blankets and try to heat them with their breath. But most severely premature babies didn't survive for more than a few hours or days. There are even accounts of desperate mothers putting their premature newborns into the oven at low temperatures.

Denucé designed the first incubator in history: a brass box with a double wall; double because it allowed hot water to be stored inside. A few years later, the gynaecologist Stéphane Tarnier hired a chicken breeder to help him design another, more advanced model. This one consisted of a thermal cot with temperature and humidity controls, so as to keep preemies in a warm, secure environment more like the mother's womb. The incubator itself was made of mostly wood and glass. The wood walls were ten centimetres thick. A lower compartment was filled with water; the baby rested on the upper one. Also on the upper part of the incubator was a glass lid that permitted doctors and nurses to view the baby without disturbing their environment. The inner thermal cot was a cushioned, insulated compartment, heated from above by an electric bulb. A thermometer tracked the temperature. It was also possible to adjust the airflow inside the incubator to provide proper ventilation, and on one of the side walls was a door for removing the baby as needed.

Thanks to this innovation, the preemie survival rate rose substantially in the maternity hospital for poor women in Port Royal, where Tarnier worked, and the incubator became an essential medical device in neonatal care all over the world.

The remarkable story of Felicia Billings takes place in 1952, in Milwaukee, Wisconsin. There are so many versions of what happened that it now seems like collective lore. Indisputably, though, this incident is another example of how, indeed, desperate mothers would put their premature babies in the oven, heeding an instinct – correctly – that they needed heat. Felicia was one such baby, weighing a mere nine hundred grams at birth, desperately vulnerable. The first thing her parents did was rush to have her christened, fearing she'd die within minutes. But she survived the ceremony. And so, arriving home with no idea of what to do next, her mother stuck her in the oven at a low temperature and took her out only to nurse and rock her. Felicia lived an adult life without any side effects.

At this moment in history, and in this hospital, and in this incubator, MyChild must have better chances than Felicia did. And so I repeat to myself: open her up, pump her up, resuscitate her. Just don't put her in my arms for me to watch her die and then watch her not dying for days, not dying, not dying, until she does, until she arrives so late to her own death that I spend the rest of my life wondering if I should have let her die in the operating room.

Anaemia. Transfusion. Tuna. I barely ate tuna while pregnant, as its high mercury content makes it unadvisable during gestation. Red tuna, the same colour as veal and other red meats. Red from iron, an essential component of myoglobin, a protein that stores oxygen in the muscles. I know this from my years of training as a swimmer, when nutrition was a critical part of my performance. I think about how all the iron on this planet comes from dead stars. The highest concentrations of myoglobin are found in the heart muscle, which requires great quantities of oxygen to meet its energy needs. This means, in turn, that the death of a star defines our heart rate, from the tranquillity of sleep to the galloping rush of love or war. If I'd eaten more tuna, would MyChild now have greater reserves of iron?

Obstetricians systematically disregard the fact that anything, or almost anything, can go wrong in pregnancy. They occupy themselves with helping us give birth to healthy infants. They treat us according to ideal scenarios. And yes, I know, the thing about the tuna probably has no bearing on reality. But the thing about the obstetricians is: at no point do they ever prepare us, not even with the vaguest hints, for the unexpected. For the possibility of birthing an unrecognisable human, or one who can't breathe. But they should, because the unexpected is hardly uncommon. They just keep it invisible.

The fluid overload in MyChild's body manifests itself in different ways, all expressing her state of perilous imbalance. MyBaby's eyes, now open when she's awake, look slightly inflamed, which indicates an accumulation of liquid in her head and brain, while her small nose looks strangely swollen, as if she had bits of cotton stuffed inside (or maybe she does and they were inserted too quickly for me to notice?). The skin on her abdomen looks taut and pink, evidence of the excess fluid pooling in her tissues. Her eyes, puffy at the moment, as if she's done a lot of crying, seem to search for a solution, and I look at her and beg her not to ask me, because I don't have it. Her breathing grows faster and more laborious, as if she were struggling under a disproportionate weight, a wooden beam that's fallen from who knows where. And her tiny limbs feel stiff and heavy to the touch, as if saturated with blood and other liquids. All of this is wrenching proof of the danger she's in, and of the urgent need to take measures that will protect her and keep her alive.

Fluid overload, I've been warned, is one of the most feared – and most frequent – complications of blood transfusions in preemies. It's often caused by the immaturity of the baby's circulatory and lymphatic system, which fights to handle the increased volume of blood and liquid it receives. The doctors and nurses are working to ensure that the treatment is as safe and effective as possible, that is, to confirm that this was the right choice. But I can barely stand the sight of MyBaby transformed into a swollen bulge.

My mother always has a perfect manicure. She says she likes her hands, everyone's always complimenting how pretty they are. She changes colours often. Good for her. I bite my nails, and sometimes I admire those perfectly paintable shapes. In recent years, I've seen my mother unmanicured only once, during my pregnancy, when I asked if we could take some selfies to remember this moment together. As if on purpose, she displays her nails in the photos: cracked and chipped and yellowed from so many years of polish and polish remover. Maybe that's when I should have sensed her malice.

There was a prelude to the bottle cap episode. I could be wrong; perhaps it wasn't a deliberate attempt to hurt me, I'm not sure, but that's what it felt like. It was a few days before. Another trip to the beach. It was August, so the place was crowded, with one peculiar exception: despite the heat, there was almost no one in the water. Besides the fact that the water was crawling with jellyfish, everyone said it was freezing. At one point my mother interrupted our conversation and announced she was taking a dip. People watched her from the shore. And then my mother called out to me from the water: 'Get in, Marina, don't be stupid, it's nice and warm!' But I was stupid, of course I was, and in spite of all the baffled stares, I followed her. The water felt freezing, just like they'd said, but since I was pregnant, it wouldn't have been the first time my body confused cold and heat. So I decided to trust my mother – the water must be fine – over the dozens of people staring as if she were crazy. I felt a shock that knocked the wind out of me, but my mother insisted: 'Come on, swim, it's good for you!' And I swam and swam so it would be good for me, and to warm myself up.

My feet were purple by the time I got out. I was afraid I'd harmed MyChild. I lay down right on the sand, no towel, to take in the heat.

I'd also been stung by a jellyfish, but before I could soothe the pain, I needed to get my body temperature back up and make sure MyBaby was still moving. Suddenly, a kick – I felt a surge of gratitude – and then another. I recognised these kicks; she was moving around in her usual way. She was fine. Safe. But now, knowing it was on a beach that her grandmother put her at risk, not once but twice, I wonder: was my mother trying to kill her there to redeem my cousin's death?

My mother has always sworn that she can weep with one eye to keep from disturbing anyone on the other side of her profile. It's another of her litanies. If I or others don't see her cry, it's because we're looking at the eye she isn't crying from. She claims to suffer in silence through a single tear duct.

MyChild, I'm going to tell you another story. Long, long ago, there was a giant called Polyphemus. He had just one eye, which was located in the middle of his forehead. He lived alone in a Sicilian cave, where he herded his sheep. One day, some strangers entered the cave and Polyphemus, corrupted by loneliness, began to eat them. But one of these unfamiliar people won Polyphemus's trust and got him to drink a lot of wine. When the drunk giant fell asleep, the men grabbed a sharp stick, heated it in the fire until it burned red hot, and cleaved it into his only eye. Polyphemus roared and shouted for help, but no one came to his aid. The men who blinded him managed to flee the cave after a few days, tethered to the bellies of the giant's sheep – so that when the sheep went out to graze and Polyphemus touched their backs to count them, he wouldn't notice the fugitives below. In the end, Polyphemus died alone in the very same cave, subsumed in darkness and sorrow.

Weeping out of one eye is impossible for a person with two. Only someone like Polyphemus could do it: one, two, three tears trickling down his forehead, reaching the bridge of his nose, then streaming down. Poor Polyphemus: so many tears for a single eye. He must have wept piteously over the one he'd lost. His weeping was so fierce that the mountains were said to tremble.

The furthest along I made it through a pregnancy was with you – twenty-five weeks – and everything was going well, very well. As the doctors assured me, everything indicated that I'd carry you to term. But then my mother appeared in the form of a bottle cap, and then you were born. And all you've done ever since is struggle. Fight. I didn't conceive you for war. I'd prepared a peaceful house for you, a place I'd built painstakingly over time. There's an American anti-war song from the First World War era called 'I Didn't Raise My Boy to Be a Soldier.' It has lines like these:

> I didn't raise my boy to be a soldier,
> I brought him up to be my pride and joy.[10]

But your grandmother had to cause me harm. The bottle cap in her mouth. That's how she placed a musket on your shoulder. All you know of her is war. That's why I sometimes dream – and I wish I didn't – that I hit her. I hit her so hard that I don't dare describe the effect of my blows, even if it's only a dream. But it's her, she's the one who sent me off to war. Who else was going to fight on your side? You're so tiny. Who else would give their life for you, throw their body onto yours to shield you from the bullets? But I didn't want to, I didn't want to. I didn't conceive you to be a soldier. I'd prepared a house and a body full of peace.

I had a friend who helped me grow up in a healthy way, and this friend had a family that protected me. We were so close that I'd go to her house even when she wasn't in and truly feel that I was inhabiting my own home. A minimal space, a humble house. The living room was a tiny square with barely enough room for a sofa and a TV set facing it. The kitchen was as diminutive as what you'd find on a flimsy fishing boat. It was the kind of house where families once shared a single living area, eventually dividing it into miniature rooms. But I loved being there. I could turn up whenever I liked, open the fridge, eat whatever I wanted. I'd take naps in my friend's bed and I liked it when she came home and woke me up.

When her family called to tell me that my friend had been killed in an accident, she was more earthly than ethereal. Not only because she'd just died, but because all the tears we wept – all of us who loved her – pooled onto her, made her heavy like stone, stopped her still. Who could ever fly with wings so drenched? And although her closed eyelids spent two more days filtering the light of two more dawns, I didn't make it to her burial in time. The layovers were short, I missed a flight. That's when I learned the world isn't small, like people claim. Anyone who says the world is small has never lost someone on the other side of it. They've never known the endless journey, autonomous as a long life, undertaken by someone travelling alone, carrying that burden while everyone else carries their luggage. As if objects were life itself. As her family and our friends grieved together, I longed to crumple in airports, in the aisles of aeroplanes; to demand solace from any stranger.

Now I invoke my friend in hopes that she'll help us. She's the most important person I've ever lost. I picture her looking down at us cheerily from wherever she is, allowing the mouths that float around her to take a little bite that will taste of things they'd never eaten – the best bread dipped in the best oil, trickled from her olive breasts, and so many other foods that shaped her body so young, because, yes, that must have been the reason for her death: to make of her and her flesh, which was always generous, a pasture for gaunt angels. What other reason could there be for such untimely deaths? I have to believe in something or I'll lose my strength. Science doesn't cut it for me anymore. Even the doctors tell me so: they keep charging me with decisions that could save you or kill you, and I have to make them by believing that something supernatural will help me, because the doctors have no idea. Even they admit it: it's impossible to know what will happen.

After my friend's death, her mother abandoned her chemo treatments and died three months later. Two months after that, her uncle hung himself, unable to bear so much loss. My friend's mother was universally beloved in town: someone who took down the dogs that hunters hanged from trees in the countryside, stringing them up with old rope when they were no longer of use to them. She'd bury the dogs whenever she could, as if she somehow sensed this was the only way she'd be able to bury the brother who would end up hanging himself for her. All three of them died from my friend's death.

The last time I visited the cemetery, I saw their graves, all lined up together in the family plot. Any stranger who goes there and sees their names would assume they suffered a traffic accident, that they all died for the same reason. And so it was. They died with my friend's death. She'd spent so many years fearing her mother's, fearing the cancer that had united us all in the struggle for hope, and in the end it was her mother who chose her own death on the night she made a pyre of her medications at her country home. Three months later, the same procession that had followed my friend – a crowd the size of the entire village – followed her mother too. The same procession with one fewer soul. That's one way to kick cancer in the teeth. Love: chemo without poison.

My mother broke the news of her friends' death to me in passing, at the end of a phone call about other completely irrelevant things. When I asked how she could tell me so glibly, she responded, 'What do you want me to say? She was more dead than alive, poor thing.'

My mother always said that my father wanted more children. She claimed she'd never used contraception because he forbade it. But I had my doubts. Regardless, in my mother's account, my father took her to the doctor to see if she was infertile. They did the usual tests and everything seemed normal. When they were alone, the doctor told my mother that she wasn't getting pregnant because she didn't want to. The insinuation – my mother's, through the doctor – was that the trauma caused by my father was so great that she had rendered herself infertile, only with him. Today I think she omitted something important: she didn't want to have more kids not only with my father, but because I existed. Meanwhile, her sister's daughter was dead as a result of her own carelessness. Maybe I was the cause of my mother's infertility.

Not long before you came into the world, a friend painted my belly to look like Planet Earth. But when you were born, that planet ceased to be an enormous sphere I tread, something external to me. Instead, it became an internal sphere that included me too. Choking on my own throat. That was the world to me when you fell into it. Pain is a hand that clutches the belly of our universe and turns it inside out: all the deserts with all their sands, all the forests with all their trees, all the fires with all their flames, are no longer on the outside, but make us into a walking vessel of plains, of roots, of contained blazes. Maybe the Big Bang was a god who exploded under the pressure of their own suffering, and that's how creation began: with the death of its creator.

I once read that 'it takes a village' to see a micropreemie through. I found this intensely moving. To me, it means you need a tribe beyond an enormous medical team; you need the support of family and other loved ones. Emotional accompaniment is as important as a neonatal cardiologist. Not only for the mother, but also for the newborn, who may tilt towards life or death in response to factors rarely considered in such cases: crooning, words, the family's nearness to the baby. Studies show that this affective ingredient marks the difference between a baby who wants to live and a baby who simply tolerates medical care – which, no matter how sophisticated, is insufficient without the embrace of a family.

For a long time, it was believed that a preemie's survival was determined by their gestational age, weight, additional complications, physical state, types of neonatal care, etc. while little to no significance was granted to the emotional side of things. Today we know that babies who live in incubators with someone always sitting beside them, reading to them, speaking to them in a soothing voice that transmits love and security, have far greater chances of survival. Family and social factors are crucial, it turns out. So how will I manage, with my cracked soul and my nappies and my swollen vagina and my aching breasts, to find the strength and words and warmth and presence of an entire village?

My friend's funeral in town was attended by eight hundred people.

I spent many years trying to get my mother to acknowledge me, trying to melt her ice. Maybe I thought, once she'd hit sixty or so, that age would thaw her, subject her to a kind of climate change. But since this didn't happen, I discovered a new fear: that after all she'd done to hurt me, I'd end up having to care for her at the end of her life. It was a real fear and easily could have come to pass. Would I be capable of *not* taking care of my mother if she got sick, or if she lost her mind and needed me? Would I be heartless enough not to bring her to live with me, tend to her in her final years, say goodbye as if I'd forgiven her? Whatever happened, I'd clearly have to care for her, and in order to do so, I'd have to behave as if the harm she'd caused hadn't marked every stage of my life and many of my decisions – the decision to move to the US, for example, and put the entire Atlantic Ocean between us, a time zone that would allow me to say when she called: *Sorry, Mama, I was asleep.* In truth, my mother rarely called, even when she knew I was sick or alone or in need of something, so many things. I would have cared for her just the same. But ever since MyChild was born, I no longer have this fear. MyBaby has cured me of it. My mother's abandonment at the worst possible times was my own business; I was the one it hurt. Her abandonment of her granddaughter is another level of pain I can't and won't want to heal – despite my newfound knowledge of a beach that has at last made everything more comprehensible. I have the right to protect my daughter with all my love, without exposing her to the wars waged by my mother for no other reason than to kill herself. No, I'm not afraid anymore: this responsibility is no longer mine to bear.

I won't be taking care of my mother.

As an old poem once said, *No la veré morir.* I shall not watch her die.

Or will I?

V

29 WEEKS

38.8 OUNCES

(A Hole in the Gut)

My then-partner and I decided to go through my second miscarriage at the country house. I didn't want to go to the hospital, although we got everything ready in case an emergency forced us to. We wanted to wait instead in an isolated spot, like a dog retreating to a box to birth her viscous stillborn pups. We laid the mattress by the fireplace and waited for the contractions to hit. The weight descended inside me like a net of restless fish, lulled by the ebbs and flows of my blood. Just two days before, this prenatal oceanography had only existed in the form of a gentle, temperate life. The temperature told me it was over. He touched me and reflexively shrank back, as if I myself were dead, unrecognisable, and he the survivor of another woman, someone stronger than I. I was cold, an unpregnant temperature, but even then, battered already by this farewell, with the flesh of our child turned against me, I pushed their father to the edge of the mattress, stuck my head under the blanket and sought his skin. I licked his back, every part of it, slowly, as if tipping water into a trough, drop by drop; I let my mouth fill with saliva, prodding my tongue from the back of my teeth to the roof of my mouth, wetting it again, then returning to his skin like a damp sponge. I grabbed his cock, tensed it towards the fireplace, waited, drew it towards the fireplace again, longer now, thickened, gesturing as it had when it flung a child into me. My lover reminded me of the doctor's instructions: 'It's important to avoid infection.' He pushed me away to protect me, or because he didn't understand what I already knew. A miscarriage: pain? Yes, lots of pain, the loss of something I would never recover, but more than that: *I'm still here*. I dripped with arousal, and it wasn't just my roiling hormones, it couldn't be only that, or could it? He insisted on being careful with me; I was enraged. Why assume I was strong enough to birth a healthy child but not get horny while surviving? That night, I learned what desire meant, and living, and dying. There would be no congratulations, no gifts, no childbirth chit-chat (fortunately) with mother-mothers, the triumphant ones who cross the finish line and let themselves have sex only when their stitches have properly healed. There would be no milk, advice, good mum exams, or visits, and for a moment I felt free; no, there would be no baby, I'd no longer suffer the agony of indecision, the terror of maybe yes, maybe no. Then something changed in my partner too: without warning, without any hint of gradual approach, he began to kiss my breasts – still swollen, still oblivious to my loss – and descended, parted my knees unflinching and looked. As he took in the sight of my dilation, I glimpsed the hole of me in his eyes, a small, dark creature snared in a trap. He rested his head between my legs and stayed there for a while, feeling the contractions against his temples, helping me, loving, lover, midwife extraordinaire, seeing me through the birth of the child who never came to know what desire meant, or living, or dying.

Due to the immaturity of their intestinal and muscular tracts, many preemies struggle to pass bowel movements on their own. As a result, they may need additional help to void their stool. Yesterday they tried to stimulate MyBaby, rubbing her anus with a Q-tip dampened in warm water, but it didn't work, so today they inserted a rectal tube to facilitate the evacuation of her faeces. (Faeces? Poo, shit – shit's better; I don't like this change in my vocabulary, this tepidness, this homogeneous medical correction). They positioned her on her side, applied a bit of lubricant to the end of the tube and introduced it into her rectum. Once properly in place, everything seemed to work: the tube began to gently, painstakingly extract the poo, the shit (faeces), the shit, the shit, the shit. Then they removed the tube with care and deposited it onto a tray. The tube was extremely thin and slightly stained. It reminded me of a stick insect. I'd admired those insects as a child: they seemed to need so little to live. Something about them unsettled me too: it's often impossible to know if they're alive or dead. A stick insect's paradox isn't its camouflage with its surroundings, but with life and death at the same time. This frightens me more than ever as I watch MyChild, stick baby.

It's three in the morning. I wake to the sound of footsteps back and forth. I see three bodies peering over MyBaby's incubator. Amanda, a nurse who looks like a teenager but whose movements are formidably meticulous, tells me that a nurse on the previous shift mentioned signs of inflammation in MyChild's abdomen, and she asked Amanda to follow up on it. Amanda agreed and alerted Dr Smith. It's true: MyBaby's tiny belly is swollen. I immediately hear voices: abdominal distension, feverishness, diarrhoea, laboured breathing, lethargy. An abdominal X-ray confirms it: necrotising enterocolitis.

It's my birthday and MyChild's tiny guts have ruptured. Necrotising enterocolitis is a life-threatening intestinal tear. Here's the scenario: the large intestine gets inflamed, and when food bacteria reach this still-immature area, the tissue gets damaged and can even die. The result: a hole in my daughter's intestine. It's a critical situation that demands immediate surgery. MyChild's diminutive form lies in the incubator with lifelines affixed to her belly and limbs; almost every part of her body is strung with a new cable (just as I'd been told: one step forwards, two steps back). I can't imagine how they're going to operate with all those cords dangling every which way. Will they have to unplug some form of essential support? To decide which of all those conduits is the least and most important? How will they open up her belly? How is it possible to cut open a belly the size of a rose? And then how will they work on her intestines? I picture them, fine as the cable on a pair of earbuds, incredibly fragile. What kinds of hands will be able to manipulate so much minuscule, practically indivisible matter? I think of children exploited all over the world, working day and night to manufacture certain garments or items that call for very small hands, very slender fingers. But a child couldn't operate on my daughter. Maybe a dwarf doctor? Is it crazy to think that hospitals should hire physicians with unusually small hands for cases like these? And why don't I see as many dwarfs – the correct term is achondroplasia, I know – as I did when I was a child? Are they more frequently aborted? Bitches every one of them, those mothers aborting dwarf foetuses who might, just might, have gone on to study neonatal surgery and work miracles on MyChild's little guts. Am I spouting nonsense? I'm exhausted. But I need to stay awake, awake, awake for the operation, to wait for the doctor when he emerges from the operating room and scan his face for the news before he can say a single word. Like in war, it's like a war, you don't hear the bullet passing through the skull; here, too, murderous words move more slowly than the gestures, the expressions of bad news. I need to stay awake awake awake after days of no sleep. Cocaine. Why don't they sell coke in hospital vending machines? Or why don't they hire someone to bite your tongue and wake you up? I'll take anything, anything would be better than this watery coffee that makes me slam the machine with rage when it's slow to come out, because I need to hit something. I need anything that will keep me from missing so much as a second of my daughter's life or death, or the transition between them.

While my daughter is in the operating room, I look up the procedure on YouTube. I wish I could avoid it, spare myself this pain, but it's like discovering a chink in the wall of a hotel room that looks onto the one next door. I'd look.

My first observation is that there are lots of hands involved. An hour ago, I was horrified to think that an adult hand couldn't possibly manoeuvre around my daughter's intestines; now it's like witnessing some kind of experiment, a furtive clinical study, rather than a surgical procedure devoted to saving her life. The lights shine on the abdomen of a miniature human being. The infant's eyes are covered and their translucent skin looks altogether transparent under the intensity of the bulbs. The music in the operating room is sinister: squealing medical instruments sing a chorus interspersed with the baby's faltering breaths.

The doctors' movements begin to follow a different rhythm: the beat of damage repair. The preemie – born at twenty-seven weeks, according to the video captions – has the same intestinal complication as MyChild does, necrotising enterocolitis, an inflammatory intestinal disease that primarily affects premature infants and is characterised by the death of intestinal tissue. 'This complication can be fatal without proper treatment' (the phrase appears onscreen in large letters). The first step in the procedure, which is called an enterostomy, is to make an incision in the baby's abdomen to access the intestines.

An enterostomy is considered a complex procedure in preemies, given the fragility of their organs and the need for fine, precise sutures to avoid any kind of leakage (I wasn't wrong about the importance of small hands and sharp minds: dwarfs, dwarfs, damn all mothers who abort their dwarfs). The surgeons must work with great care to join together the remaining segments of the intestine and avoid further complications.

During the operation, the premature infant is sedated, but their tiny body shifts around a bit. I know those movements, or some of them: it's like when MyChild moved inside me, the little spasms I suspected overtook her as she slept. Now all foetuses look alike to me, as does the suffering of all mothers.

It's time: the surgeons open up the baby's miniature belly with the meticulousness of an explosives expert neutralising a bomb. They peel back the layers of skin and muscle until they reach the damaged part, revealing the inflamed and punctured intestines. Even I can tell: it's obvious that they're inflamed and punctured, a senseless jumble. The more inflammation there is, the more complex the operation, as the intestines may literally come apart in the surgeons' hands. When they locate the segment of intestine that's afflicted by necrosis and needs to be removed, they perform a 'bowel resection' (words onscreen) by extracting the damaged tissue and deftly stitching the healthy ends together to restore intestinal function. The baby is so small that they're little more than a lump under the sheets as the doctors and nurses work to repair the harm.

At the end of the video, the following text appears:

> The surgery took place in an operating room specially equipped for premature infants and performed by a multidisciplinary team of expert neonatologists and paediatric surgeons. The premature infant was closely monitored during the entire procedure in order to detect any changes in her vital signs and administered a combination of anaesthesia and sedatives to keep her immobilised and avoid any pain or discomfort. After the surgery, the premature infant was transferred to the Neonatal Intensive Care Unit for close supervision and the administration of antibiotics to prevent infection. Fortunately, and despite the urgency and complexity of her condition, the surgery was a success, thanks to the hard work and dedication of our medical professionals.

Video with a happy ending. But MyChild is still on the operating table.

In our situation, 'success' isn't quite so simple. For preemies, life may reign one day, but then the next day death takes the lead, and I'm up in the stands, screaming like a fan to cheer on life, which now must catch up with death, reclaim the baton.

To a preemie, the word 'success' is something like the five minutes of fame allotted to even the most mediocre individual. Speakers blast whoops and applause, and then the person goes home and commits suicide, because they know there's nothing on the horizon but the same depression as always, maybe the chronic kind, and five minutes of fame only means five more minutes of life. After that, all bets are off.

One day, I was having a late-afternoon snack with a friend at her place when someone knocked on the door. It was her boyfriend's best friend. I didn't hear a single word of what he said before my friend punched a window and shattered it. Then she collapsed onto the floor, glass and all. She'd seen it in the messenger's face. Her boyfriend had suffered a fatal motorcycle accident. The words came later, but they no longer served any kind of informative function, only filled in the details of his death. The details. That's how it usually goes: language is slower than the expressions that precede it.

Dr Truong emerges from the operating room. Not a single lock has shifted on his impeccable head of hair. I can tell from his face. My daughter is alive: five minutes of success, and then more, there will be more, I'm sure of it. She's survived. She's alive. Her tiny guts have been repaired. I get up and hug the doctor, wordless too.

Amanda came in with incredible news: tomorrow, when you'll be twenty-nine weeks along, they're going to start 'kangaroo care'. They'll bring you to me naked except for your nappy and place you on my chest, skin-to-skin, your ear resting against my heartbeat – so that you'll remember the sound, the one-note concert interrupted too soon for you.

Apparently it's been proven that this marsupial warmth, this cardiac music, complements the technology used in the neonatal units of many countries, optimising chances of survival and reducing hospitalisations. But I find myself thinking of elephants, not kangaroos. Baby elephants orphaned by poachers can't sleep alone. In many elephant sanctuaries, caretakers spend the night embracing the little ones, sharing a blanket, bottle-feeding them every three hours. In many cases, milk alone won't ensure their survival; it has to be accompanied by a spirit of care, making them feel safe and loved. I've never seen a premature elephant baby. Their skin can't be so fine. A delicate kiss surely wouldn't leave a bruise.

I'm thrilled but also terrified. Terrified that my body won't be as efficient as your glass urn. After all, my raw little love, my body couldn't shield you from shock, couldn't keep you inside me until you were finished forming. I linger on this detail too: they'll bring you in wearing only your nappy. I had clothes at home for you, clothes for babies who make it to term, who are born when they're supposed to. If you survive, I won't be able to dress you in them for three more months. It's not a lot of clothing, but I'd carefully selected every set of pyjamas, every pair of socks, every hat, all folded and stored in a wardrobe just for you. I think you'll like them. But you have to live if I'm going to dress you.

Then I'm reminded of my first roommate here in the hospital, the cuddle cot, her baby's refrigerated body, the saddest flash fiction of all time:

'For sale: baby shoes, never worn.'

The first thing that comes to mind, after the excitement of realising I'll get to hold my daughter in my arms for the first time, is disinfection: the protocol I'll have to follow before I can touch her. In my case, it's more complicated. I've suffered from obsessive-compulsive disorder since childhood, though I've had it under control for years. By 'under control', I mean I no longer devote most of my day and my energy to elaborate verification rituals, as I did when I was a teenager. I'd get out of bed countless times to check something, anything, over and over again, which meant I barely slept. By day, the situation wasn't much different. I remember one morning when I was getting ready to leave for university. Since I'd been cleaning the fridge and had just adopted a puppy, I got it into my head that the dog might have slipped into the fridge without my noticing and frozen to death. I turned back, went into the flat and opened the fridge door. The dog wasn't there; in fact, I could see him in his bed under the kitchen table, watching me with tensed ears. I left again, ready to go to class – but at the halfway point I thought maybe I hadn't checked closely enough, I'd been distracted, better look again, and so I retreated once more, following the same sequence: I opened the fridge, made sure the dog wasn't inside, looked at the dog under the kitchen table, repeated to myself that everything was fine. But no, once again, I had to turn back, and I repeated the whole thing so many times that in the end I simply stayed home: I wouldn't have made it to even my last class of the day.

I used all sorts of methods to mitigate my disorder, mostly without medical assistance. There's one thing I learned and always try to keep in mind: in my view, this disorder is like any other addiction. That is, the only way to keep from relapsing is to go cold turkey on your rituals. I have to stay in bed no matter what, even if I'm convinced a gas leak will blow up the whole building. I can't go home even if I think my dog is dying of hypothermia in the fridge. I won't wash my hands five times in a row, counting first to forty and then to thirty and then to twenty and then to ten and then to three. Whenever I find myself standing at the sink, I limit myself to washing my hands just once, because there's a fine line between one and five and thirty times a day. Scrubbing – the strict hygiene protocol applied by surgeons before an operation, one I'm also supposed to follow before I enter the NICU – has restored my hand-washing addiction with a vengeance, both in the hospital and outside it. This is the protocol that's yanked me back into my endless mental loop:

Before I go in to see my daughter, I have to wash my hands with soap and water, rubbing them for at least twenty seconds, fingernails and wrists included. I wash them for sixty seconds, rest for five seconds (it needs to be exactly five), then repeat.

Then I have to wet my hands and forearms with hot water and apply antiseptic soap, including nails and wrists once again, then scrub for at least two minutes, using a special brush for my nails. Here, too, I double the duration of the process.

Rinse with hot water.

Dry with a disposable paper towel.

Pull on sterile gloves.

The whole process can take up to an hour. Even so, I'm still terrified that I won't be clean enough to keep MyBaby safe.

I know I'm just another ridiculous addict, trapped once again in the spiral of my mind. It'll be hard for me to return to one (just one) hand-wash when I'm back home. While chances have increased that my daughter will join me there, only one thing is certain for now: I've already fed the monster of my disorder, and the more I feed it, the worse it gets. It's all well and good for me to tell myself that I'm doing all this to protect her from contamination, but once I'm back in my flat, I'll be capable of doing it even if she's crying with hunger, exhaustion, or pain.

Lo and behold, the obsession persists at home. I step into the shower and apply the routine to my entire body. My skin is dry, since I don't want to use any kind of lotion that might disrupt the sterile atmosphere at the hospital. I implore the deities of any religion that requires hygiene before prayer to protect me. Water as a purifying agent is important in many faiths. I need the great polytheistic miracle, and I feel that it's coming to pass: a god with a thousand compassionate mouths has kissed MyChild's tiny forehead.

Your body on my chest, your skin against my skin. I feel the weight of you – I didn't think I'd feel it, but I do, just enough for me to feel protected too. You've come back to me. You look at me, clutch one of my fingers. Hard. You're strong. I close my eyes and try to fight it, but I start to cry, so much that I fear my heart-beat will speed up and upset you, but no – Katy points to the monitors, which I can now read like a pro, and I see the mathematics of my motherhood in its figures: my skin has sparked a series of physiological reactions in you. Your heart rate, which accelerated slightly when you were lifted out of the incubator, has stabilised. Your breathing deepens and evens out, and your body temperature instantly steadies with my skin's natural heat. Before she leaves us to ourselves, Katy whispers, 'This intimacy and skin-to-skin contact is the best thing for her neurological and emotional development.'

And before she steps out, I ask, 'Can I give her a kiss?'

'Yes, you can.'

Now that I'm holding you in my arms, I'm surprised at how unafraid I am of contaminating you. I kiss your hands, your forehead, your feet. Fuck whatever bacteria might live in my saliva. Nothing that comes from me can harm you. It's not an intuition. It's a certainty.

Instantly, you fall asleep.

Instantly, I fall asleep.

Every day for the past week, I've admired how you slumber in my arms. I live to hold you. I notice the grams of weight you're gaining. I notice every change, almost all positive now. At this very moment, as I look at you, I think about how you're the only person who's seen the place where your siblings lived. I rock you to the sound of your own breathing, make up lyrics to well-known melodies, and ask you as I sing if you ever saw one of them, even as a shadow, in my uterus. BabyOfMine, let me tell you another story: when the US dropped an atomic bomb on Hiroshima, the temperature at the site of impact approached the temperature on the surface of the sun: four thousand degrees Celsius. Men and women pressed their hands into their eyes to keep from losing them. The people closest to the new sun vanished, but not entirely: they left the silhouettes of their bodies behind. Outlines filled with nothing. Atomic shadows. Look, little one: a child leaned against that wall (shadow of his small hand), a dog sat on those stairs (shadow of its pointy ears and tail). There was a mother who thought she recognised her daughter's shadow against the wall of a school. She devoted the rest of her short time on Earth to preserving this silhouette, sheltering it from wind and rain, like someone protecting a cave painting – the final pose of a gazelle – at an archaeological dig. After the explosion, a man recalled later, he was surprised to see a woman wearing a very tight kimono. Then he realised that she was actually naked, so naked that not an inch of skin was left: the radiation had stamped the flowered hues of the fabric onto her body.

My body was emptied of life not once, but twice. And by the time I should have been emptying myself of a whole, living life through non-premature labour, my mother shook you out of me. She was the pilot who dropped her bomb and fled, not even bothering to witness the explosion in her wake.

But I fill gaps and imagine things, wondering what happened when I was sedated. I see radioactive glimmers that show me, when the light hits, the shadows of your siblings; I see us all for a few moments, as lightning illuminates a dark field. MyChild, will you tell me if their shadows still mark the walls of my womb? I wish I could hug their outlines, the ones that only you, and only maybe, have ever seen. I carry them with me like atomic shadows, filled with void. Carried. Carried. Not anymore. Ever since you've recovered your shape, ever since you've taken on the state of a recognisable baby who will surely survive, those shadows too have filled with flesh and skin.

Let's make plans. We'll go to the Golden Gate Bridge, the famous San Francisco landmark. Every year, dozens of people select it as spot for committing suicide. On-site cameras document these deaths and occasionally manage to impede them. There's a photo of me on that bridge, but I'm smiling. I'm pointing to Alcatraz Island, from which I swam out to the San Francisco coast the next day. The water was the coldest I'd ever swum in. Before I began, I was warned that the surf might obstruct my view of land, I should bear this in mind, and if that happened I should remember that I wasn't alone, the boat accompanying my route would always have its eyes on me. I should internalise these words so I could find them when I panicked: even if I thought I was alone, even if the waves concealed solid ground and I was certain I'd been shipwrecked in a frigid sea, many people – all invisible to me – were keeping watch. I made it to the coast without much trouble, and later someone mentioned a news story from the day before: a man had thrown himself off the Golden Gate Bridge. A note was found in his pocket: 'If one person smiles at me on the way, I won't jump.' I'd always clung so obsessively hard to life that I didn't need the smiles of strangers to save me, to reach out and grab me at the last minute and halt my plunge into the ocean, hard as cement. But I still think about him today, and there's something in that pocket, that note, that bridge, that speaks to me. There's something of my plankton-woman-self that casts a light on the bridge, glimmering from the waters of these adult coasts. And even though I don't yet need a stranger's smile to save me, even if you flounder through your artificial gestation, if your heart should stop, there's something of myself, inexplicably broken hips, missing tendons, a being-adrift in spite of myself, without a note, without pockets. Me, a womanless woman, me, who will go with you, halted in my arms, to the bridge, golden and indecisive. Yet every time I hold you to my chest, I feel sure this won't happen. One day we'll travel to San Francisco, and we'll smile at everyone we pass around the bridge.

We'll cross it three times. Three at least.

'Kangaroo care' has brought MyChild back to my body; it has restored something, however small, of what nature had prepared me for. But it also comes with new responsibilities. Now that I know how to hold her and can actually do so, as long as the figures on her monitor are stable, I must also learn what to do in the event of her frequent bradycardias: when my daughter's heart rate falls and the alarms beep louder, when her heart tilts towards the fateful 'zero'. I must learn to do it well before I leave the hospital, the doctors insist, because this could just as easily happen at home.

The alarms beep and beep. A nurse rushes over and observes me, vigilant, as if I were a medical student on rotation. The first thing I have to do is wait a few seconds to see if MyChild manages to stabilise on her own. If she doesn't, and if her heart rate keeps dropping, I have to sit her up and pat her on the back and on the chest, breathe into her nostrils, reminding her heart to beat normally. It has simply forgotten: it needs to be reminded. This is another state of normalcy that cuts me to the quick each time. Yes, bradycardia can be rectified with a few little pats, but I can't be lulled into thinking – just because the solution is normally simple at this point, now that my daughter is stronger – that the problem isn't serious. What happens when her heart slows down and the alarms go off is that my daughter begins to die. It's 'normal', yes, but terrifying. It doesn't mean that there's anything wrong with her heart. It's just another lapse in her immature body: a lapse that, if unattended, becomes fatal, irreversible, in a matter of seconds.

They assure me that episodes of bradycardia will get less frequent and less dangerous, and so far it's true. Still, I'm not less afraid than I was before. In fact, I'm more afraid. More, because the more strength and life and future I see in my daughter, the more I have to lose if it all vanishes.

I'm going to tell you another story. A man is sentenced to starve to death in prison for a crime he didn't commit. He's allowed a single visitor, his daughter, on one condition: she can't bring him anything to eat. Time passes, and when the man shows no signs of advancing towards his final sentence – that is, death from lack of food – the warden gets suspicious. He can't figure out what's going on, because the man's daughter never brings any kind of food on her visits, as he himself ensures each day. One afternoon, the warden decides to spy on them. That's how he discovers what's going on: the daughter, who had given birth just weeks before, is nursing her own father at her breast.

Instead of being scandalised, the authorities take this act as a symbol of what would come to be known as Roman Charity and grant the father his freedom: a father transformed by his daughter, through 'charity', into her child.

Over the past weeks, I've felt as bad as I could possibly feel: like an old man and a lonely woman, or like a lonely man and an old woman, two sorrows of different genders, the kinds whose very difference causes friction. A square, rusty wheel in the soul.

But now I'm feeding you. There's breastmilk in your belly, ChildOfMine, as much of it as you want, milk straight from YourMother. But I can't forget how, for a few crucial days, it was another mother's milk that fed you, a mother to us all, an earth mother. She nourished you when I couldn't, and we don't even know her name or face. I wish I could build a monument to that anonymous mother who feeds other mothers' children, like the she-wolf who nursed Romulus and Remus. A monument to the woman who starts an entire civilisation: the mother to those who manage to survive, and thrive, despite their own mother's drought.

Soon after I was born, my mother told me, I vomited blood. The doctor determined that the blood actually came from my mother's breasts: she had mastitis. She started giving me formula. I was always surprised to know that my mother and I, at least for a few days, were united beyond pregnancy. My mouth at her nipple. But the beach, that beach, grows more and more present in this story – my story – and I can better perceive the mother she was before my cousin died. Before what she became.

There's something else about my childhood that my mother does remember, although in this case I remember it too, so her own memory doesn't contribute much. When my cousin died, my mother gave me a toy: one of those wooden boards with multicoloured cylinders that pass through the board when you hit them with a little hammer. I can imagine the scene. Let's say I'd just nailed in a blue piece and continued with one of a different colour, blow by blow, piece by piece, disappearing from one side, then reappearing on the other – all the colours, all the wooden pegs that were once living parts of a tree.

I'd spend hours hammering away at that toy, one side at a time. This, my mother said, is what made it possible for her to get things done, as long as she could hear the noise of the hammer. If she didn't, then she'd come in to see what I was up to, why I wasn't banging at the cylinders round the clock, as I was apparently supposed to do to keep from bothering her.

When I got pregnant with you, I remembered the toy and rescued it, or it rescued me. That's when I understood what motherhood meant to my story: recovering, in one fell swoop, the power that had been drained from me since my own first day of life. It's about giving birth and welcoming newborn flesh by replacing all the tongues that ever silenced me. It's about receiving a hammer on the same day I gave birth and reclaiming the visible part of the game. It's about extracting – one hammer-blow at a time, like a sculptor in a trance – the shape of a blood-borne power that my mother tried to take away from me.

When my mother decided to leave this hospital and abandon us both, she walked out through this door: third hell on the right, furthest to the back. The door for the ones who don't want to leave. But now that I've learned more about what used to be our family's silence, I'd reach out a hand to show her the way. She just needs to want me to. Doesn't she?

VI

31 WEEKS

52.9 OUNCES

(I Choose Blindness)

An incubator fulfils the basic functions of the uterus, but the most important part is missing: liquid. Throughout my time here, I've constantly pondered alternatives that might allow micropremature infants to survive. I'm sure we all do. As if saving the future could save us from the present. Obviously, my scientific knowledge in this area is nil. But I spend my sleepless nights scouring the internet, and I learn that someone before me – someone with the actual skills to do it – has nursed the same fantasy, which turned out to be viable. They named it the 'biobag', also known as a 'biocontainment bag' or 'artificial womb system'.

As far as I know, one of the most significant landmarks in biobag research came about in 2017, thanks to a team of foetal researchers at the Children's Hospital of Philadelphia. In their study, the researchers placed eight premature lambs, which had been surgically removed from their mothers' wombs, into a sealed bag filled with a special liquid that simulated amniotic fluid. The lambs were extracted at an age equivalent to twenty-three weeks of human development.

The biobag is an innovative receptacle made of hermetic polyethene that provides a sterile environment for the circulation of synthetic, antibiotic-enriched amniotic fluid. It also allows for the elimination of waste. The amnioinfusion employed in the Philadelphia lamb experiment involved a solution specifically designed for this purpose. The artificial amniotic fluid included a mix of nutrients, lipids, proteins, carbohydrates, electrolytes, amino acids, and other essential components to supply an appropriate environment for the development of the foetus, imitating the chemical balance present in amniotic fluid.

The researchers connected the blood vessels in the umbilical cords of the eight premature lambs to a specialised pumpless oxygenation device. Rather than relying on an external pump, the lamb's own heart propelled the flow of blood around the device, emulating the natural rhythm of foetal circulation between the foetus and the placenta in utero. This direct connection avoided pressure imbalances in the foetus's heart and blood vessels. What's more, immediately introducing the lamb into a closed and fluid environment presented the changes that normally occur when a newborn takes their first breath: the act of filling their lungs with air reorganises their circulation, redirecting the flow of oxygen through the lungs instead of the placenta via the umbilical cord. By contrast, the biobag allowed foetal circulation to continue without the foetus having to breathe through their still-immature lungs, preventing numerous serious complications.

After five weeks of experiments, the lambs managed to survive in the biobag for a four-week period. During this time, the researchers observed the continuous development of their organs and systems, including their lungs, brains and digestive processes. The lambs also practised breathing, just like human foetuses do in their mothers' wombs. They grew wool, their eyes opened. Their whole development seemed to coincide with what they would have experienced if they'd remained in utero.

The objective of the study wasn't to achieve the lambs'

long-term survival in an artificial environment, but to prove the viability of the biobag as a possible support system for premature foetal development. Which means that the lambs were slaughtered after those four weeks and extracted from the bag for subsequent analysis.

Five thirty-one a.m. I search YouTube for the words 'lamb', 'premature' and 'biobag', and a link to a video appears. The lamb is inside a bag of liquid, fitted quite tightly around its body, like one of those frozen vacuum-packed bags, but larger and full of conduits connected to the outside. It doesn't yet have any wool, at least not visibly so, but I can clearly make out its eyelashes. Its eyes are shut. It seems to be sleeping, but it moves its legs, its ears, as if dreaming. Instead of an umbilical cord it has a large catheter hooked up to a machine. A voiceover explains that the machine serves as the placenta, which exchanges carbon dioxide in the blood for oxygen. It seems to be developing without pain, without suffering. It's calm, existing in an environment that looks far more natural than an incubator.

Like lambs dreaming in bags of artificial amniotic fluid.

When we dream, humans experience life in the most isolated and mysterious of ways. 'All men whilst they are awake are in one common world,' wrote Plutarch, 'but each of them, when he is asleep, is in a world of his own.' How much more inaccessible to us, then, are the dreams of animals?

I'd like to tell you about my grandfather Juan. There are things I hope you'll learn from him through me.

He taught me to raise myself in the countryside; to pluck hearts of palm from the earth, peel them without hurting myself and eat them on the spot; to look for scorpions and avoid getting stung when I played with them; to orient myself with the stars; not to cry when I got bitten by a bug or aggressive dog; to catch snakes; to find water; to sleep in the grass; to treat my stings in the hours when the toxins are strongest. My grandfather Juan opened the doors to all the fields of Andalusia before me. Certain episodes are especially vivid to this day: for example, we often found eggs I incubated without knowing what they'd hatch, because my grandfather never told me. I loved awaiting the surprise of a new life, wondering whether it would greet the world with a trill or a slithery hum. Once, transporting one of those little eggs to a different kind of sand, I dropped it. The shape that emerged wasn't fully formed, but I could already tell it was a lizard. I must have been six or seven. It grieved me to see the tiny animal on the ground, enmeshed in green gelatine and surely suffering. I ran and flushed it down the toilet, fervently hoping it was an amphibian.

My second memory is of an enormous injured box turtle we rescued. We planned to return it to the countryside once it had recovered, but one day it fell off the balcony. I dashed downstairs and found its shell completely shattered. The turtle writhed, and I thought and still think it was looking right at me. It was incredibly heavy, and it seemed to weigh more from being broken than from being alive. Once again, I felt the lancing pain for another creature. Not knowing how to ease its anguish, we put it in the freezer.

My third memory is of an injured vulture. I refused to leave its side until it was collected by workers from a wild animal preserve. It scratched up my hands. I'll never forget the smell of it: like wheat. That's what the plumage of birds of prey has always smelled like to me. Today, when farmers burn field stubble in Seville, I catch the scent of vulture feathers.

My fourth memory is of a water snake that swallowed a frog right in front of me. I knew it was the law of nature – my grandfather told me so – but I couldn't help from squeezing the snake's belly so it would spit out the frog. I broke the only laws I respect. Today I'd like to break almost all the others. At least I saved a frog.

My fifth memory is of a small rat, also injured. Caught in a downpour, we found it waterlogged and inert. We dried it off with a hair dryer and it slowly came to. We gave it shots and put it in a cage, waiting for it to make a full recovery. I was probably about eight then. I'd stick my finger into the cage and the rat would bite me. 'You're not a bad rat,' I'd tell it, and then I'd stick my finger in again, and the rat would bite the open wound. I always offered it the same finger, as if a different finger would make for a different rat; I wanted this one, not a different one, to change. I bled heavily and still have the scar. Again and again and again went that finger into the cage as I repeated the same thing each time: 'You're not bad.' Maybe I hoped these words would make my wish for animal virtue come true. And I still hope my words, which never changed the rat, can change me for the better. I still cultivate scars. And sometimes I bite. But I'm good, MyChild. YourMother is good.

In one of few childhood photos I still have, I'm standing at the entrance to an aquarium. It's from one of those museum photo services: they take your picture on your way in so you can find it on your way out, displayed alongside hundreds of other photos of seemingly happy families. I'm wearing a ridiculous dress – it looks more old-fashioned than something my grandmother would have worn – and holding my mother's hand. My legs are twigs, another reason why I always hated dresses. I was so bony that my classmates were always making fun of me. My mother's response to my shame: 'Don't worry, you're going to end up fat like your aunt and grandmother when you're older, and then all you'll want is to slim down.'

We were living in Tenerife and we'd gone to Loro Parque for an orca show. I was about ten years old, and already found it absurd that such a large and powerful animal was made to do silly stunts. The orcas' pirouettes, the trainers' routines: I didn't find it entertaining at all. As for my mother, all I remember is her single-minded fascination with a one-armed trainer; she was sadistically obsessed with the limb that one of the orcas had torn off. 'Look, look,' she laughed, 'the whale got his arm, the whale got his arm!' Her laughter was like the sound a flea-bitten dog makes when he scratches himself. Of course, my mother was utterly indifferent to the suffering of the orcas themselves, which by then was common knowledge and the cause of widespread protest. As for me, I was still oblivious to the issue of animal abuse; I simply didn't like the show, with the mindless applause and gesticulations of adults and kids alike. I've never visited an aquarium again, but if I could go back today with my mother, I'd throw her in and put her right in view of the whale. Look, Mama, I'd tell her:

Here's an eye more formidable than your head,
a heart that weighs two hundred pounds,
a heart bigger than you are.

Today I know that some of these whales wind up as inmates in whale prisons in Russia. For the first few months, they don't want to eat, they don't move (they don't know how to move without their pod); they hang suspended in the water like stalled Zeppelins. They cry their shrill, incessant cries. Listen, Mama. Listen with water in your ears. They haven't stopped crying since they were trapped in nets and airlifted away, frightened of the helicopter blades, the landscape down below, the blue-black expanse of a home whose depths they believed in, their eyes glassy from the wind. A half-litre tear. So you could mock them, they were struck until their dorsal fins dropped off with sorrow. Instead of living the hundred years they're supposed to, they'll manage four or five, or twenty-five (if their luck is poor), or they won't live at all. In many aquariums, they're locked up from five in the afternoon to seven in the morning, confined in the dark, in metal containers no larger than a whale-sized coffin. They go mad.

MyChild's incubator sometimes reminds me of a fish tank.

Mama: my daughter's tiny heart is bigger than you are.

The lingering presence of foetal cells in the mother's body after birth is known as 'microchimerism'. They can survive in the mother for decades, sometimes for her entire life. Although the phenomenon isn't yet completely understood, scientists believe that these cells can migrate from the placenta to other organs, including the heart, liver, and brain, incorporating themselves into the mother's tissues and establishing connections with her immune system.

Just as dark matter is invisible to us but present all over the universe, my foetal cells remain in my mother's body, hidden to the naked eye but present in their essence. Just like dark matter, which seems like a dark void but exerts a powerful influence on the movement of visible matter, such cells may have an unconscious influence on my mother, shaping her personality, her way of being in the world and being with me.

Yet I find neither solace nor protection in genetics. After everything that's happened, I struggle to imagine that something as intimate and sacred as a cellular connection could exist between my mother and me. Just like dark matter, cellular chimerism evades any rational explanation, leaving me with nothing but unanswerable questions and a sense of wonder in the face of an unfathomable universe I now no longer even care about. Maybe the stars only explain that love and genetics, at least for me, aren't always aligned.

For some reason, it's widely believed that preemies, if they survive, will develop faster in an incubator. False. Until the forty-week point, they grow more slowly than the normal rate according to their gestational age. All of their organs are still developing, a process far more difficult outside the womb. One day's growth and development in utero is equivalent to three days in an incubator. And as for the brain that makes us so uniquely human, this develops mostly in the final months. Between weeks twenty-eight and forty, the foetus's brain triples in weight. MyChild, who has now spent a month outside me, turns twenty-nine weeks today. The future of her brain is still a mystery.

Ever since MyChild opened her eyes, she seems more and more solid, more certain in the way she directs them, although I've been told that her vision is still developing. The maturation of her eyes is a natural, gradual process that continues even after birth.

I think again of all the times my grandfather would come into the kitchen at the country house and all of us cousins could instantly tell what he'd done: got rid of the kittens born to a feral cat on the property. The rule, as I've said, was to slaughter them if they were still too small to open their eyes. Sometimes the mother cats would hide their young, and my grandfather would find them a couple days later, when their eyelids had already parted. Too late. Then he'd come into the kitchen and announce, 'They opened their eyes.' My grandmother wouldn't say a word, just look resigned. But the youngest among us were thrilled, because we knew the kittens were still alive, and we'd get to watch them grow up and join the dozens of feral cats who had opened their eyes in time to be saved.

I'm pretty sure the medical team taking care of MyChild believes, at least some of the time, that I'm on the verge of losing heart. I'm not, or at least I am less than before, when she seemed so much weaker and I thought that one more hour of her survival meant another hour of loving her and dying myself, dying deeper, dying more fully; one hour more than the infinite nothingness of all other deaths. Still I think, although I can't be sure, that some mothers and fathers really do find themselves giving out, because other relatives appear beside some of the incubators. If I get worn down, no one else will keep MyChild company. At the very least, I've been making sure to eat well and drink lots of the protein and vitamin smoothies that are often offered to patients who have lost their appetite in chemotherapy or other treatments. I drink them to strengthen my body and to produce more milk.

The unexpected, the dreaded. Again.

Apnoea.

For some reason, it's the worst she's had so far.

She isn't breathing.

Resuscitation.

Her body slack. Again.

Blue.

I count the seconds. I die with each and every one.

Her colour returns. She's alive. Again.

'It's normal,' they repeat. 'It's normal.' And those two words open the door to another meaning I haven't let inside for days: it's still normal for your daughter to die.

They increase her oxygen supply. Sometimes you think a remedy is only that: support, forms of aid, like oxygen in this case. MyChild needs more oxygen so she can breathe. Right. I can't imagine anything counterproductive about oxygen. But it's not so simple in the realm of micropremature infant care. The babies' retinas haven't developed yet, so they lack the capacity to produce certain protective enzymes and antioxidants. When administered high concentrations of oxygen to treat respiratory problems, prolonged exposure to this oxygen can generate free radicals, unstable and reactive molecules that may damage the cells and tissues of the eye. This, in turn, may cause retina damage to or detachment – or even blindness, in certain serious cases.

Once more, I must choose. I curse this freedom. I think: *My blind daughter*. OK. Blind. She'll still be able to live a happy life. Just save her lungs. As if for reassurance, they tell me about a technique called 'controlled oxygen', in which they try to maintain the concentration of oxygen at a safe level, then gradually adjust it as the baby develops. Although, they emphasise, there are risks.

Now I understand why a paediatric ophthalmologist comes in every day. No matter. Even if she's blind, may she never lack for oxygen. I can't understand all these balancing acts. Being alive and being dead. Being dead and being blind. I feel like I've been forced to juggle on a cursed tightrope.

And still, at the end of the day, for every decision I have to take with or without the doctors' help, I realise there really is a place where I find balance, a place that takes the edge off my anxiety when I need to choose between two options, or three, or five, all with their own possible and fatal consequences. Two questions. My balance hinges on two questions:

If MyChild ends up blind, will she be able to love?

And I answer myself:

Yes.

And if she ends up blind, will she be able to be loved?

And I answer myself again:

Yes.

If both answers are positive, then that's the right decision for me.

Blindness.

Blindness.

I choose blindness.

Yesterday, I thought I caught a flash of concern in the ophthalmologist as he checked MyChild's eyes. Today, though, he didn't hesitate to mention a new operation: retinopathy surgery. I kept quiet, but I felt dizzy. As soon as everything seemed stable once again, something new has appeared, something I can't even make sense of. And it requires another operating room. I long for a helping hand, a loving touch, someone else's concern. I take in the doctor's diagnosis: 'Your daughter's retinas have been damaged.' The explanation: the blood vessels in a baby's retinas keep growing after birth to reach the areas in need of oxygen and nutrients. If the baby is born before the blood vessels have finished developing, they can grow abnormally, which sometimes results in retinopathy – especially if large amounts of oxygen must be administered to the infant. So what I've feared has come to pass: in needing to receive supplemental oxygen to improve her breathing, she's suffered retinal damage. What's more, the bulbs used in light therapy to treat neonatal jaundice give off a blue light that can also harm babies' retinas.

'When is the operation?'

It's always the same answer: 'As soon as possible.'

Everything is as-soon-as-possible here. God forbid that MyChild should die and can no longer be operated on. Sometimes that's exactly the feeling I have:

that micropreemies exist for operations. I know it's not true, I don't want to sound ungrateful, but I never have time to process the haste to open up MyChild's body, her organs.

A few days ago, I learned that one of my dearest friends had died. Under these circumstances, I don't even know what the news is doing to me. But when I think of him now, it's in the form of this cliché: 'Wherever you are, help me!'

I met Gastón in my PhD programme. I was cursing my bike lock in Spanish; it had gotten stuck and I'd been struggling for half an hour to open it. Overhearing me, he stopped and said unprompted that some locks yield if you pour a little Coca-Cola into the keyhole. He spilled a bit of the drink into the metal hole, and the lock opened as if by magic. Everything was like that with Gastón. Life smoothed itself out in his wake. It took him twenty minutes to edit essays it had taken me days to write. He was famous all over campus: in a seemingly effortless way, he'd solve people's problems and still manage to be the life of the party. He became my swimming buddy. We'd swim together because the seemingly tireless Gastón did sometimes get tired. His back hurt not from his poor posture while studying, but from the weight of other people's burdens.

Gastón decided to go home to Argentina when he finished his PhD. 'Don't be stupid,' we all protested. 'With a brain and a CV like yours, there's a brilliant future awaiting you in New York.' It was precisely because of his intelligence that he wanted to return to the countryside, resume rural life, buy lots of cows. I mourned his absence, but he never abandoned me.

I hadn't replied to his last text: I'm often slow to answer the people who matter to me most, because I like to have the space and time for it. How could I have known that, in the intervening weeks, the gears of my friend's life would slow until they came to a halt at the base of a cliff? He'd fallen asleep while driving. Maybe dreaming of his herd.

'Hi beautiful,' his emails always began. They always ended in the same way too: 'I'll send you a plane ticket whenever you like and you can come take a break in Patagonia.'

Patagonia, along with my friend Gastón, was the place that beckoned whenever New York started to wear me down. Generally in December or January, when winter, like depression, begins its slow corrosion; when it feels like it will never end.

The few times I leave the hospital to shower at home or bring back clean clothes, I stop at a beauty salon in our neighbourhood where a dog is always napping in the doorway. I love to pet him. That first day, the owner glanced at me from inside and smiled.

'What's his name?'

'Gastón.'

Gastón. The second Gastón I've ever met.

Yesterday, Gastón wasn't there when I walked by. He'd died of old age, his owner said. She tucked him into his bed the night before and felt his heart beat for the last time; he died in the company of his most beloved human.

After hearing this story, and after all the time I've spent feeling guilty for not answering Gastón's email, I feel like I can finally rest. I'd like to think that the dog's heart contained my friend's heart too; that my own Gastón spent years sitting in the doorway of the hair salon as I stroked his fur, thinking about how he shared the name of my saviour in Patagonia, not yet feeling – until today – that my touch was the reply I owed him. That's how generous Gastón was. Capable of waiting patiently day after day, sitting there like a sick old dog until I saw my chance to say goodbye. I trust that he'll find it easy to help us. We won't even need to believe in God.

In Dr Truong's office, five people explain how the retinopathy surgery works: Dr Truong himself, the ophthalmologist, an anaesthesiologist I don't know, a nurse I also don't know, and Adrianne, who gifts me a moment of physical contact whenever she's nearby – an affectionate squeeze of the arm or a pat on the back so gentle it's like a caress. Sometimes she cradles one of my hands in hers.

It's a delicate procedure (that's the first thing they say, 'a delicate procedure', which I think is overkill; I take it for granted that everything is delicate around here). The operation will be performed inside the incubator. MyChild will be sedated through a face mask, which will administer a combination of anaesthetic gases and oxygen. They'll use a laser to burn the abnormal blood vessels in her retinas. The process may take up to an hour, depending on the number of blood vessels in need of treatment (this sounds like a positive sign to me; an hour isn't much). Then they trot out the risks: infection, haemorrhage, retinal damage, adverse reactions to the anaesthesia. I also take for granted that behind each of these words they call 'risks' is death.

My mother doesn't remember much about my childhood, as I've said. And so, even if we do rekindle our relationship, she won't be able to tell me much – which means, in turn, that I'll have no way of knowing if my daughter's behaviour is anything like mine when I was a child. I do know from my mother that I used to make up words she thought were clever, like the one I mentioned earlier: 'I'm going to tank you. I'm going to flush you down the toilet and then I'm going to drain the tank.' I can't be sure, but I imagine that this was around the time when my sorrow and frustration at my own invisibility began.

I'm reminded of something that happened three years ago, when I had my first miscarriage. My mother was at a spa and not always able to pick up the phone, because her massage appointments couldn't be rescheduled. My foetus, tiny and round, fell right into the toilet bowl. But I didn't tank it. I put it in a little box where I kept the few rings I owned and buried it under a flowering almond tree.

Not to worry, said my mother when learned I'd miscarried, *it must have been very small, it was nothing.*

That was the word she used: 'nothing'.

I buried nothing, a nothing with five fingers, measuring just a few millimetres on each hand, and five on each foot. I counted them.

I buried a nothing with an umbilical cord and a head the size of a raspberry under a flowering almond tree.

This hospital has a psychological support group for mothers who have lost, or are losing, a baby. There's another for the women who'll have to spend the next few months beside an incubator. When I woke, I found a pamphlet on the bedside table: a guide for family members on how to support mothers at this time. The whole medical staff knows I'm on my own, so I imagine that the pamphlet must be a matter of protocol; surely they left it for me while I was sleeping to spare us all the discomfort of putting it in my hand. It recommends that relatives read to the baby, take photos to share with the mother, keep the rest of the family updated, let the mother vent, feed her healthy food she likes (including the occasional unhealthy treat), and – this is presented as the most important recommendation of all, in boldface and repeated several times – remind the mother that it's not her fault her baby was born premature. I know it would do me good to have someone attending to all these things, except for the last. I know perfectly well that this isn't my fault. It's my mother's. At least I've got the most essential kind of support, the one the professionals have emphasised in bold: not blaming myself.

VII

32 WEEKS

65.9 OUNCES

(Plane Crash)

Today has dawned on another empty incubator. But I know we'll be out of here soon, and alive. Both of us. I don't feel a trace of survivor's guilt, the syndrome that so often afflicts people after a traumatic experience. In truth, I know little about this syndrome; I've heard it mentioned sporadically over the years, but I never understood it, maybe because I never tried to learn more. In any case, now that I've witnessed the occasional emptying of other nests, I still don't. Will I understand it in a few days, once we're back home? Will I feel guilty for the fact that we've both survived? Will my waking hours or my dreams echo with the first words I heard when they wheeled me down the hall ('We're going to try to save them both')? Will I feel at the least as if I should have died in compensation for the life and long future of the baby born to another, younger woman who, according to the logical order of things, deserved to live more than I did?

For now, no, I don't feel guilty. Although of course I do die a little, or a lot, when another child's light goes dark. Sometimes I lock myself in the bathroom and pound the walls, like in those movies in which someone, usually a man, smashes his fist on something until he bleeds. Then I take some toilet paper and wipe the wall, not out of any great respect for cleanliness, but to distract myself from hitting again. Cleaning instead of counting to ten.

However I end up feeling later, I've started to imagine

joy, a future with my daughter – and maybe some side effects, it's still too soon to say, but a future with happiness in it, or as much as anyone else is capable of. Of course, it's not all good cheer ahead for us. I do wonder how I'm going to explain certain things. My mother, obviously. My mother. Her grandmother. Where is her grandmother? Who cares if I ask myself this question; sooner or later, my daughter will be the one asking. And where is everyone else on my mother's side of the family? Of course we still do have relatives who love us, but others vanished with my mother. My cousin's death scattered us like a grenade. Many still bear the shrapnel. Many of the women in our family separate early from their children. They leave. How will I explain so many absences to my daughter? And I write to her, try to write her something, things, experiments, rehearsals for how I might tell her. Should I say they all went out skiing one day and an avalanche hit and trapped them and they're still buried under the ice? But skiing where? No one would believe that in a country with so little snow. Besides, there's no way the old women in our family would go skiing, it's utterly implausible. I think up all kinds of nonsense. But after so much trauma, after believing that our life together was over and then realising it wasn't, that we'll manage to go on, I have to get myself moving again, thinking, writing. Maybe a plane crash?

I think about how I'll tell you someday,
when you find the language to ask,
about my mother, your grandmother,
and part of her cursed lineage.
It occurs to me that the most practical thing
might be the briefest, most irreversible scenario:

a plane crash.
I'll tell you something like:
My darling, my mother's side of the family died
while travelling to . . .
Where?
To a wedding?
Whose wedding?
I'd have to think.
That's the least of it –
they simply burned to a crisp
between the blazing fabric of the seats
and the molten metal.
I laugh at the thought:
it's an idea as ridiculous as it is efficient.
Maybe I'll think about all this sometime
in the future
when I'm sitting on the front edge of a rowboat
before jumping into the sea.
It'll be during peak cuttlefish season
(clandestine fishing, obviously)
because that's when they mate.
Snorkelling, suspended at the surface,
I'll watch them down below,
two or three metres down,
alighting on the bottom
like a large maple leaf
covering a smaller one.
I'm good at this, my daughter,
I'm silent, patient,
I hear my steady breathing
as my eyes seize on the perfect spot
for my harpoon to cleave,
cut short their copulation,
male and female skewered on a single stick.

You'll see, my girl, as I saw the first time
I did it,
that their ink drains as they're brought to
the surface,
the blue ascent goes dark,
my hands are blurred.
Once out of the water,
the ink keeps sprouting from its siphon
in a tower of liquid black
as petroleum.
I get ink in my mouth and spit it out,
as if I were just another cuttlefish.
Inside the boat, I remove the rod
piercing both their bodies,
hard bodies,
still pressed to life,
and their yellow eyes with black
horizontal pupils stare at me
like exhausted sheep,
and they start to drowse,
as if they weren't moving towards death
so much
as towards extinction.
The boat will rock in the blue I've pulled
them from
as the cuttlefish cough, heaped in the
plastic bucket.
And there we'll be, my daughter, you and I,
the warm night seeping in,
and we'll sway
as the sky begins to spatter itself with stars
like luminescent fish
snagged on the hooks
tossed down from a still plane

in the air.
I think:
there's a cursed artery in your grandmother's
liver,
there's cowardice,
indifference to her daughter,
to her granddaughter,
and your grandmother is in that motionless
aeroplane,
a plane ready to crash as soon
as I'm strong and ready enough to tell you
that there's no more grandmother in your
grandmother.

Another story: a long time ago, in a place called Lumbini, Nepal, a prince named Siddhartha was born. His father wanted him to inherit his throne, and he overprotected his son as much as he could. For many years, the child never left the palaces, devoting himself to a rigorous education in the arts, sciences and sport. However, his studies concealed the existence of poverty, illnesses, and other sad but inevitable facts of life. So Siddartha grew up thinking that everything beyond the walls of his environment was just as rich and gratifying as the narrow world he knew. Until the day he decided to escape, when he encountered all the ugliness that had been hidden from him. He saw a leper and asked his servant what it was, and when he was told, he asked if this disease could affect just anyone. Yes, it could. And little by little, he discovered the full scope of human misery. He never returned to the palace, and he dedicated his life to searching for the root of suffering in hopes of healing it.

MyChild, I want to tell you about this city, because you're a little like Siddhartha: you've been isolated, hyper-protected in your glass cot. I'm telling you to spare you a shock when you're out, and to keep you from telling yourself: All that care, all that effort to keep me alive and get me home, and now I have to fight more out here than when I was inside.

I'd heard from my grandparents about infestations in Spain (bedbugs, which prompted the evacuation of whole tower blocks). But the first times I wandered New York while pregnant with you, I was struck by another kind of excess. I'd never noticed it before: toys abandoned in the doorways of people's houses, or on the pavements. MyBaby, some are practically new. There are also cots, pushchairs, car seats, baby walkers, even unused breast pumps. Sometimes a sign accompanies these objects: 'Free, New' or 'Gently Used'. They usually end up on the street after making the rounds on social media or charity websites, with the invariable caption of 'Free for the first person to pick up today, we're out of room.' In this city, after all, there's not enough space for so many people. Flats are mostly very small, unable to adapt to the ever-changing needs of an ever-growing baby: if they need a bigger cot, you have to get rid of the smaller one, and fast. If they no longer fit in the car seat you struggled to save up for just six months ago, you have to give it away before acquiring a new one. As a result, wandering certain New York neighbourhoods means wandering a landscape of abandoned toys, along with everything else that doesn't fit anymore, and which ends up in the shopping carts of homeless people, who try to figure out how to sell it.

Rats and baby supplies wherever you look. And trash, MyChild, lots and lots of trash. There are no trash cans in Manhattan. Starting at four in the afternoon, neighbours gather their trash bags and deposit them on the sidewalks. Remember, if you're going to walk around Manhattan, you need to get used to the sight: sidewalks heaped with bags for collection by city garbage trucks, hours or days later. Among many other consequences, the accumulation of trash bags means a feast for rejoicing rats.

Far sadder than new, abandoned toys: hundreds and hundreds of people sleep on the street as if they themselves were trash.

Rats, toys, people flung into a state of squalor and neglect. You'll see. There's some of everything in this city. But I promise you that once we get out of here, I'll show you both the beautiful and the ugly. This world that protects you now – it's not the world.

VIII

35 WEEKS

89.5 OUNCES

(The Bath)

In the emotional passageways of the Neonatal Intensive Care Unit I now know all too well, MyChild has been trapped in a kind of contract, subject to the requirements that condition her release: her independence from the monitors, the vote of confidence that her lungs will be able to handle a freedom we'll experience as a kind of probation. To get out, MyBaby must be able to perform certain functions without any kind of specialised assistance, and to meet several physical requirements:

Reach the minimum adequate weight for her gestational age (in her case, five and half pounds).

Feed adequately, whether with breastmilk or formula.

Maintain her body temperature without the controlled environment of the incubator.

The absence of serious medical complications such as infections, cardiac or respiratory problems and neurological disorders.

That said, these requirements don't guarantee her long-awaited liberation, however diligently fulfilled. We'll only be able to breathe a sigh of relief when she turns one year old, the essential milestone that will finally allow me to say: *My daughter has survived her birth.*

Sudden infant death syndrome is voracious in preemies, although it's delicate as a flower petal: silent, treacherous.

The good news is: fuck sudden infant death syndrome, we'll deal with that later, I'll hire a sentinel if necessary, for when I pass out from exhaustion. Our home awaits us, and today we know that our departure from the hospital is imminent. We know because Dr Truong himself, visibly excited by what it means to a mother to hear what he's about to say, has asked me: 'Do you have your car seat ready?'

All the other mothers in earshot burst into applause. Installing a car seat is the best news a doctor can give you in here: a passport to life. And the doctors themselves are genuinely moved to deliver it, because they know that what they've given the babies who make it out of here could mean eighty, a hundred years of living. No doctors can offer a greater life expectancy than those who work with premature infants. They too are expectant. They're women. They're mothers.

Adrianne's face shines as she comes in. She hands me a small sponge, makes her way over to MyChild, and says, 'Don't tell me your mother thought of bringing you home without a bath!'

Of course I knew I'd have to bathe her eventually. Of course I had lots of questions about when and how to do it. But I have so many questions about so many things that I didn't think this one was a priority. It's a surprise. A gift.

MyChild reacts with a gesture that makes me laugh, as if she'd understood: she opens her eyes as wide as she can, makes a little sound and bows her head. I think that this moment – yes, this one – must be the happiest of my entire life. I feel the way other mothers say they felt on the day their babies were born. Here it is now. MyChild's first real bath: this is my full-term childbirth. MyBaby is fully made.

Adrianne brings her to me. There haven't been any cables for days, just a nasal cannula that doesn't seem to bother her. Now I'm a mother with a babe-in-arms. A baby who looks like a baby. A mother who looks like a mother. Alive. Both of us. And we head for the bathroom with Adrianne. There I watch the process she teaches me to repeat at home:

She wraps MyBaby in a towel, bundling her up like a spring roll, arms against her body.

She uses a thermometer to check the water temperature.

She brings MyBaby's back, all bundled up, into contact with the water, and starts to rock her gently from side to side, introducing her horizontally until the water covers her whole body except for her head.

She gestures to a small towel on a tray and tells me to clean her face without soap, just water, very delicately.

I pick up the towel, which is pleasantly warm, and draw it softly across MyBaby's forehead, around her eyes, from tear ducts to the outer edge, around her mouth. MyChild sticks out her tongue, as if wanting to suck up the water. She definitely looks like a baby. I keep washing her face with great care. 'Time to wash her hair,' Adrianne grins.

She rocks and rocks my daughter, who seems quite comfortable. No, she doesn't seem: she really is. She's my daughter, I know her by now. She's happy, relaxed, enjoying this moment. It's special for her too, sensory, pleasurable.

I use a bit of soap to wash her scant, fine hair. It floats in the water like gauzy strands of wool. Then I rinse it with a bit of water from the tub, cupping it in my hands. I feel like I'm christening her in my own atheistic way;

I'm not just washing but purifying her. At last. At last: it's time for me to name her. I'll think about this later.

Then Adrianne explains that I should unroll her bit by bit and wash her whole body with soap. First one leg (after drawing back the towel), then the other, then her tiny bottom, her tiny belly, one arm, the other arm, her chest, and so forth, always re-covering the area we've just washed. Finally, my spring roll is completely enveloped again in her warm, wet towel. Adrienne continues to rock her. The very last step is to remove the whole towel and keep her body in direct contact with the water for a few moments.

We dry her, put on a fresh nappy and dress her in her pyjamas. MyBaby is asleep by the time her little hat is on.

The happiest day of my life.

My water birth.

And I think, inevitably, of the beach. Not the beach where my mother shocked me into labour, but the other beach, where my family gathered to spend a Sunday together, thirty-six years ago. I remember some of the food we brought with us. The watermelons we buried at the water's edge to keep them cool with seawater. I went to check on them from time to time; it made me feel important to be the guardian of something. I also remember moving away from the shoreline so I could dig a hole deep enough for water to well up. I enjoyed this particularly: not digging close to the sea, where the water darted forth right away, but farther out, closer to the pine grove, where I had to use a shovel and dig for a long time before I caught a glimpse of pebbles, then larger stones, and then, once I'd pulled them out, a little water, then more and more. It made me believe that I'd be able to find water anywhere. In the desert, say, like in the adventure films and survival stories that filled my head. When I got tired, I'd lay a towel over the hole and cover it with sand for camouflage. Then I'd call for someone in the family to come see, and if my prank was successful, they'd step right into the hole by mistake. I loved pranks. In any case, I remember all sorts of things, including my mother, as I've already said, an excellent swimmer, teaching me to dodge the blows of the waves, diving in when the largest ones came at us. I liked looking up at the wave from below, and I felt safe there with my mother, who'd grip my hand hard, both of us holding our breath until the wave had swept over us and broken on the shore, white and foaming. My mother was beautiful then, even other women in bikinis complimented her body, she was eye-catching, and she loved me. Every day until that day, just a few hours later, she loved me. If I'd had a watch, I could have marked the exact time when I disappeared for her, which was the same time as my cousin's disappearance. When she woke up and slipped out of my sleeping mother's arms, maybe as a kind of game, and made it all the way to the pine grove without anyone in the family noticing she was gone. I'm not sure if I don't remember her because I was so young, or because my memory did me the favour of erasing her so I wouldn't blame her for my mother's lack of love for me.

We step out of the lift. There's a murmur as we make our way down the halls, a gentle sound swelling into a clamour of emotion. It's the applause of doctors, sanitation staff, and patients gathered on both sides of the corridor to say goodbye. I think what I thought every time you were in surgery: at that moment, all your doctors were focused on a single life. Your life. This time it's different, though, because it's no longer just your doctors. The news has spread that a micropreemie – the one nobody thought would survive – is going home today, and other specialists, other technicians I've never seen before, have joined the celebration. They're not taking care of you anymore. They're admiring you.

Before I place you in your car seat, I look back, and up, and take in the high-rise hospital building whose role I share: Mother. You're the daughter of many. I'm no longer ashamed, and I no longer believe that my body failed. Daughter of many. That's a gift I'd never imagined. Daughter beloved by so many.

Maybe your vision will be damaged and you'll have to wear glasses from a young age. Maybe you'll always be the shortest child in your class. Maybe you'll experience more complicated side effects that the doctors can't anticipate yet. Or maybe you'll grow up like any other little girl. But no matter what happens in a future that remains entirely uncertain, one thing is for sure: I can say an emphatic *yes* to the two most important questions for any human being.

Can you love?

Of course.

Can you be loved?

More than anyone in the world.

Notes

Unless otherwise stated, the works cited below were translated from the original Spanish by the translator.

1 Some of these images are drawn from Sonali Deraniyagala's testimony in her book *Wave: A Memoir*. New York: Vintage, 2013.
2 All quotes or paraphrased passages from Sy Montgomery are from her book *The Soul of an Octopus: A Surprising Exploration into the Wonder of Consciousness*. London: Simon & Schuster, 2015.
3 *Life Is a Dream*, Pedro Calderón de la Barca, (1629–1635)
4 I learned a lot about Urbach-Wiethe disease thanks to a book by Henry Marsh, *And Finally: Matters of Life and Death*. London: Jonathan Cape, 2022.
5 'El lagarto está llorando' ('The Lizard Is Crying'), Federico García Lorca, 1927
6 *Yerma*, Federico García Lorca, 1934
7 Excerpt from 'Ah misery, my mother tears me down' from *Uncollected Poems* by Rainer Maria Rilke, translated by Edward Snow. Translation copyright © 1996 by Edward Snow. Reprinted by permission of North Point Press, a division of Farrar, Straus and Giroux. All Rights Reserved.
8 *Mars*, Fritz Zorn tr. Robert and Rita Kimber, New York State: Knopf, 1982
9 *La mosca*, Slawomir Mrozek. Madrid: Acantilado, 2005
10 'I Didn't Raise My Boy to Be a Soldier', Alfred Bryan, Al Piantadosi, 1914

Also by Marina Perezagua

The Story of H, Ecco Press

Also translated by Robin Myers

We Are Green and Trembling, Gabriela Cabezón Cámara, Harvill Secker

Pedro the Vast, Simón López Trujillo, Scribe

Death Takes Me (co-translated with Sarah Booker), Cristina Rivera Garza, Bloomsbury

Restoration, Ave Barrera, (co-translated with Ellen Jones), Charco Press

A Father Is Born, Andrés Neuman, Open Letter Books

Akoya Publishing
222 Kensal Road
London
W10 5BN

First published in Spanish as *La Playa* by Pre-Textos

First published in the English language by
Akoya Publishing Ltd in 2026

Paperback ISBN 978-1-83675-008-6
Ebook ISBN 978-1-83675-020-8

Design by Holly Titchener
Text design by Phil Cleaver
Typeset in 10/13pt Egizio URW by
Six Red Marbles UK, Thetford, Norfolk
Printed and bound in Lithuania by BALTO print

FSC www.fsc.org MIX Paper | Supporting responsible forestry FSC® C107574

1 3 5 7 9 10 8 6 4 2

A CIP record for this book is available from the British Library.

The authorised representative in the EEA is eucomply OÜ Pärnu mnt 139b-14 11317 Tallinn, Estonia.
hello@eucompliancepartner.com
+337 576 90241

akoyapublishing.com